D.E. Malone

COFFEE LOFT
SERIES

A Cafe Au Lait Kind of Love
Copyright © 2024 D.E. Malone
All rights reserved.
Cover designed by Beck and Dot Design
Library of Congress Cataloging-in-Publication Data has been applied for

For exclusive content and book news, subscribe to D.E. Malone's *Welcome to the Sweet Life* newsletter.

1

I *magine your ideal coffee shop. Does it have a fabulously inventive menu? An atmosphere that speaks to your soul? Or maybe the staff are so awesome that "only cool people need apply" was probably in the job description. Coffee Loft in Greenhaven is a choice spot to unwind and refuel while enjoying its happy, caffeine-infused vibe. Owner Ginger has created the perfect café for brew-minded customers. From the friendly staff to the adorable mug wall for returning patrons, Coffee Loft is my ideal place to visit with a friend while I sip my latest favorite drink. This Quad City gem is dog-friendly, too! ~ Café Lover*

Ginger Giatti dipped the frother into the cup at the back counter while rereading the Yelp review on her assistant's phone. She'd post this on the website as soon as she found a spare minute. In the meantime, she and Merris tended a last-minute rush for drinks before the storm hit.

Outside, the western sky looked like a bruise. Roiling gray clouds churned closer by the minute.

"This is one of the best reviews we've ever received." She finished the drink, snapped on the lid, and called out the name she'd written on the cup.

"I figured you'd be thrilled," Merris said as she worked on several iced drinks. "Wouldn't you love to know who it is?"

"It could be anyone." She took a clean mug from the rack to start a latte.

There was nothing like a rave review to end the work-week. Primed to lock the doors promptly at eight, she had a busy night ahead of her. With a girlfriend visiting whom she hadn't seen in ages, her to-do list was as wide as the Mississippi River across the street.

Merris glanced over her shoulder. "Should I ask Jace to wipe down tables? I think he's about finished with dishes."

"Good idea. I bet we won't have many more come in tonight with the forecast." Someone exited the shop, and through the opened door, the sky rumbled in agreement.

Merris frowned. "We should probably stack the outside chairs, too. The wind is really picking up."

"Why don't you tell Jace to do that, too, please."

Twenty-something Merris was Ginger's hardest-working barista. She entrusted Merris to run the café on days when Ginger took off. It wasn't like she was far away if Merris needed her in a pinch anyway. Once she bought the building, Ginger quickly renovated the apartment above Coffee Loft for herself. It was one of the historic brick storefronts in the Olde Towne District of Greenhaven. The building had good bones, the contractor had told her. She was lucky to own it.

Merris finished her drink order then went to check on Jace in the back kitchen. Ginger started the latte for the next customer. Behind her, chatter in the busy dining area slowly ebbed as customers left due to the incoming late summer storm. Chairs screeched across the tile floor, the doors opened again, her flag outside snapped in the wind. She lifted the pitcher of steamed milk to finish off the delicate heart design of the latte art.

WOOF!

Ginger jumped, the pitcher wobbled, and the cute little heart was now drowned in a soup of steamed milk. Some even dribbled over the rim, pooling onto the saucer.

She grumbled under her breath, ditching her efforts for the finishing touch.

"It's your friend," said Merris with a sarcastic note of cheer in her tone when she returned from the kitchen. "Should I ask him to leave?"

"I hate to do that. He's one of our most regular customers." She eyed the man who'd appeared on the patio despite Stormaggedon bearing down on them. "I'll take care of it."

"Maybe you should rethink the dog-friendly policy." Merris glanced over her shoulder and toward the shop window. "That dog he has with him today is more horse than canine."

"Right? I think his bark just rattled the mugs on the mug wall. No joke."

She chanced a look at the front window again. Cal Donner had kicked up his feet on one of the chairs, raking his thick, dark hair with one hand and hanging onto the leashed

3

horse-dog with the other. The thing pawed at one of two women who sat at the table next to him, vying for their attention. They laughed, and even from a distance, Ginger could tell they were flirting with Cal. It grated on her nerves, the way women swooned in his presence.

The overhead lights blinked as Ginger handed the latte to the young woman who'd ordered it, then made her way from behind the counter and out the front doors. Cal spotted her as soon as she stepped outside. His overeager expression always made her smile in spite of herself.

"There she is," he crowed. "How's Ginger today?" Cal flashed her a Hollywood grin, which she'd quickly learned wasn't reserved only for her. His charm was a part of his wardrobe. She bet he even smiled in his sleep.

"Hi, Cal. You're keeping a different schedule today. You usually come *before* lunch on Fridays." She eyed the two women at the other table. They tossed their cups into the garbage while casting furtive glances at the two of them.

"Schedule change. I had a load of work to finish up," he said, rubbing the dog's neck as it leaned against him. "Hey, I want you to meet Ridley. He's my new foster."

Ginger stuck her hand out to let Ridley sniff her. The dog offered a lick, leaving a gooey trail of drool across her palm.

"Ridley, so...nice to meet you." She wiped her hand on her apron. The dog was so large his nose almost reached her chin with his four paws on the ground. "What happened to, ah, Gipper?"

"Gunther. Adopted yesterday," Cal said. "I still think he would have made the perfect boy for you."

"My cat would not appreciate me bringing a dog into the

mix." How many times had she mentioned this? She'd never been a dog person. "Was Ridley crossbred with a Clydesdale?"

"Part Dane, part shepherd," Cal said with a laugh. "Isn't he a handsome boy?" This he cooed in a baby voice, going nose to nose with Ridley.

Goodness. Cal needed to take this love fest somewhere else so she could get the patio in order.

"Looks like we're going to get some rain. I don't want to kick you out, but I think we're going to stack the chairs so they don't end up down the block."

"Sure, sure. Can I get an iced Loftie to go?" He slipped a ten-dollar bill from his shirt pocket.

"I'll be right back with that," she said, just as a gust rattled the flag pole above her head.

Grumbling, she left him on the patio to go make his drink. Inside, Jace wiped down the tables in the empty dining area. Merris pulled the garbage bag out of the container and tied the ends together.

"Any luck?" Merris asked.

"He's still here, isn't he?"

Merris giggled. She'd teased Ginger before about Cal coming in not only for his almost daily coffee. *He watches you when you're not looking,* she'd said. It was nonsense, of course. Her indifference probably challenged him is all. He was the type who loved basking in everyone's attention. But Merris didn't buy that, especially on the occasions when he'd leave behind cute little notes on the table, like "thanks a latte" and "you mocha me want to come here every day." Ginger just rolled her eyes when Merris presented them to her, and she teased her right back. *No, they're for you*, Ginger would insist.

Overhead, the lights blinked again. The hum of the equipment quieted for a second, then surged to life again.

She exchanged a look with Merris.

"Maybe you should head home. I'll close up." She looked over her shoulder to where Jace had just turned over the last chair and set it on a tabletop. "Jace, you too. I don't want you two to have to drive through the storm."

"Are you sure?" Merris said.

"Positive."

"Aww, look at that. He's stacking the chairs for you," Merris said, nodding to the patio.

Sure enough, Cal had tied Ridley to the wrought-iron railing so he could gather the chairs together. He lifted one in each hand, whereas she could only do one at a time.

"I think he just earned his drink," Merris said with a wink.

She huffed, but silently she agreed. She'd give him the drink on the house for saving her time. *Surely, he wouldn't read into that, would he?*

As she pulled down the last set of window blinds, someone's opened umbrella skittered down the sidewalk. One of the patio chairs Cal hadn't stacked yet toppled over. He glanced at her with gritted teeth, mouthed "yikes," then ducked when one of the metal poles from the awning above his head clattered onto the sidewalk. The poor dog tucked his hind end, ready to bolt, but Cal unwound his leash from the railing. She motioned for him to come inside. It was getting scary out there.

Cal pulled open the door, bringing in a burst of wind and rain just as the storm hit.

"This will blow over in a few minutes, I bet." She stepped back from the window and looked down at Cal's wild-eyed horse-dog, the poor thing.

Cal knelt down and pulled Ridley close. "It's okay, buddy. You're okay."

The lights blinked in rapid succession. The dog whined.

"Here, this is on the house. Thanks for stacking the patio chairs." She handed him the drink and his money. She glanced overhead at the light fixtures. "I sure hope we don't lose electricity."

She'd barely finished uttering those words when, sure enough, the lights flickered again.

This time they went out for good.

2

Best cup of espresso I've ever had! And bonus, they stock their pastry case with cider donuts from Apple Hill Farm! ~ Never2MuchCoffee

Cal temporarily lost sense of his surroundings when the lights blinked out. Ridley tugged against his leash and whined, so Cal wound the strap around his wrist one more time for good measure. He hugged him against his leg, giving the dog's side a reassuring pat.

"That's just perfect," said Ginger, somewhere near him. She'd moved, and now her voice was muffled.

"With the wind blowing like this, it was bound to happen. Do you have a flashlight?"

She fumbled with something before the beam from her phone flashed across his face. He blinked, temporarily blinded.

"Sorry," she said. "Now what am I going to do? I haven't even cleaned up yet."

The outline of her body slowly came into focus against the thin rays of light showing through the closed blinds. If it weren't for the power outage, now might be the perfect time to take their customer-slash-coffee-shop-owner relationship to the next level. He'd been dying to find a crack in her no-nonsense armor. Maybe ask her to lunch. They could grab something from one of the food trucks parked near the outdoor mall. They could sit on one of the benches alongside the street or by the fountain and finally get past the small talk. And this time, he wouldn't bring one of his fosters. Ginger might even flash that megawatt smile at him for real, instead of her all-business version. Actually, either one jump-started his pulse rate...

"Cal."

After all, how often was he alone with Ginger? Never.

"*Cal?*" She pointed the flashlight beam at him again, this time on purpose.

He startled. "Yes?"

"If you want to go, I understand," she said. "I'll let you out and lock the door behind you."

"I can stay. Ridley's already settling down." He tried blinking away the spots swimming before his eyes, but no luck.

"I should probably report the outage first, right?" she said, looking around the dark café.

"That's a good idea. Then turn off anything that was on. The power surge might hurt your equipment when every-thing comes to life all at once."

"Good thinking," she said. She headed toward the counter. "*Oh!*"

Ridley yipped. Metal legs screeched on the ceramic tile floor as Ginger bumped into a table and ricocheted off of a free-standing display shelf. Several things landed with soft *thuds* onto the floor. Catching herself against the counter, she pointed her flashlight to the floor where bags of coffee littered the area around her feet.

"Are you all right?" It wasn't so dark that he couldn't see the annoyed look Ginger threw Ridley's way. "He's scared or he wouldn't be sticking so close."

"I'm fine," she said curtly before taking a deep breath. "I'm sorry, I just hate storms."

He picked up the coffee bags and arranged them on the shelf while Ginger called the power company. Beside him, Ridley panted. Cal put a hand on his head, then pulled the dog against his side again. The front doors rattled with a gust of wind, and even with them closed, the scent of wet earth drifted into the shop. More rain was on the way. As much as he wanted to stay and help, Ridley's nervousness might be too big a distraction. Now behind the counter, Ginger answered questions from an automated phone system, then hung up again.

"How about I follow you around with your phone as you shut off everything."

In the dim light, she nodded. Her jaw was firmly set. Now he regretted not leaving when she'd come outside before the wind picked up.

They walked behind the counter, unplugging the machines, then headed through the kitchen and into the back office. He angled the phone at each of the outlets and light switches as they spotted them.

Outside, something crashed on the sidewalk. A thud against the building reverberated through the floor. The tornado siren blared to life against the backdrop of pounding rain and wind. Ginger looked toward the ceiling.

"I sure hope my windows are closed upstairs," she muttered.

"We're in a tornado warning. A little rain inside your apartment might be the least of your worries."

Ridley let out a long, mournful yowl. The look on Ginger's face told him the situation was getting worse by the minute.

"We should stay back here in the office. It's the safest place without windows," he offered.

She nodded glumly.

Their phones simultaneously beeped a weather warning, and Ridley's howls kicked up a few decibels. Ginger leaned against one wall and slowly slid down to a sitting position, looking defeated.

"You should probably get down here, too. In case the building collapses," she said dryly.

She kicked her legs out and crossed her ankles. When he didn't move, she patted the floor next to her. Ridley took that as a sign of encouragement and tried to park his hind end on Ginger's lap. Cal quickly pulled the dog to the other side of him. He joined Ginger on the floor.

If she doesn't hate me by the time this is over, there's hope for us.

"Is he always this skittish?" Ginger asked.

He put a hand on Ridley's neck. The dog shook with fear. "He's actually pretty chill. Great Danes can be big loafers."

"I guess I can't blame him. This is some storm."

Her features softened as she looked at them. She didn't seem as uncomfortable in such close quarters as he expected. Maybe there *was* hope for them.

"These rescue dogs are a mystery sometimes. Their history, what they've been through, isn't always known when they come in to the shelter."

She clucked her tongue. "He's lucky to have you."

Cal bit the insides of his cheeks, a habit he had when he felt self-conscious. Ginger didn't hand out compliments often. When she did, they carried a lot of weight. His insides turned to gelatin on those occasions.

Even cocooned in the dark office, the sound of trees thrashing and rain beating against the windows competed with the siren. And underneath it all, a low, ominous hum came to life.

"Do you hear that?" she asked. "It feels like everything is vibrating. Like a train rumbling by."

Cal did hear it, and while he had his suspicions, he wasn't about to tell her a tornado might be bearing down on them. His throat constricted as he gripped Ridley's leash tighter. He'd experienced one once before, growing up in rural northern Iowa. Not directly, but he'd seen the funnel from a distance when the finger dipped into the farm fields, the dust cloud it kicked up, and the aftermath when it hit one of the tiny nearby towns. It was something he hoped never to experience again.

"Not sure how much good it will do, but you might want to duck under your desk," he said.

Ginger turned toward him. "What are you saying?"

"I think that's the sound of a tornado. It may be just the funnel cloud passing overhead. Or——"

Ginger popped up and made a futile attempt to yank all six-foot-two inches of him off his feet, too.

"I have a better idea," she said, tugging his hand again. "There's a shower in the back corner. It's safer."

He pulled Ridley through the narrow space of the office, following Ginger's faint form ahead of them. There was a tumble of boxes, a louder crash, and Ginger crying out for the havoc she wreaked in the dark room. Again, her phone light blinked on, lighting the path for him. She ducked into the standing shower, squeezing into one corner when he and Ridley joined her. Hunkering down to the floor, they listened in silence to the roar growing louder by the second.

"If I live through this, there's going to be one heck of a mess to clean up," she said.

"If I live through this, I'll help." *And ask you out to dinner, too.*

Something crashed into the lobby with the sound of splintering glass.

Ginger groaned. "I'm going to take you up on that."

3

"Coffee, sweets, ambience. Need I say more? Five-plus stars! ~ Graham H.

Outside, the howling slowly died down. It was hard to gauge how long they'd taken shelter in the back room. Ginger didn't want to think about what she'd find in the front of the shop once they came out of their hiding place. Getting out of this shower stall and away from Cal and that tongue-lolling, hot-breathed monster was her first priority, though. Her hip pressed dangerously against his despite squeezing herself against the wall as tightly as she could. The sensation was annoyingly pleasant.

Something wet touched her face. She yelped.

"Did you just lick my cheek?"

"*What?!* Of course, I didn't." He snickered. "I can't believe you just asked me that."

"It's not funny. And neither is that dog's breath."

"Don't be offended, Ridley. She's just having a bad day." Cal's voice cracked like he was on the verge of laughing.

"This can't be fun for you, either. Sitting in a dark shower stall on a Friday night, when you could be lounging out on the patio with your fan club." She felt a smile transform her face too. Cal's struggle to keep from laughing at her comment was contagious.

"As a matter of fact, I'm having the time of my life," he said brightly. "Fan club?"

"They're not?"

"Dogs, by nature, are very affable, social—"

"I'm talking about the people drawn to you whenever you bring one of your furry friends."

He sighed. "Dogs naturally attract people—"

"And dogs especially attract *females*, it seems." She said it with a note of humor, but the constant crowd around him made her uncomfortable. He was the life of the party; he loved the attention. Especially *female* attention. It hit a little too close to home.

Cal snorted derisively. "Not all females."

This was true. She wasn't about to dispute it.

"Your silence is deafening," he said flatly.

"Well, that's because I'm kind of a cat person."

"I'm sorry."

"I happen to think it's a virtue."

He snorted.

"What?"

"Nothing. Nothing at all," he said with a hint of sarcasm.

The guy was infuriating. Sooo good looking, but infuriating.

Cal eased himself and Ridley out of the shower stall and dusted off his pants. He extended his free hand toward her.

She reached up, thankful that the noise, inside and out, had quieted, and now she could assess the damages. But when Cal's grip swallowed her hand and he pulled her to a standing position, her thoughts scattered like leaves in the wind. She stared dumbly at their intertwined hands even though she could barely make out their outline.

Cal had frozen, too. The battery-powered exit sign above their heads caught the glint in his eyes. They were almost as big as Loftie lids.

"I, uh..." he stuttered.

She yanked her hand away, brushing it against her skirt. "Thank you," she managed to say. Her pulse rate galloped like a racehorse. *What is wrong with me?*

"We should go see what survived," he said in a husky tone.

"And what didn't." Ginger shone her phone's flashlight around the office and headed out into the lobby, needing to put a little space between her and Cal.

Even with the power still off, the lobby was strangely bright. A simple explanation about why the light was different became apparent right away: a large branch lay inside the vestibule between her dining area and the sidewalk.

It had broken through both doors. Outside, one of the redbud trees on the sidewalk had snapped off at the trunk. Branches and debris from fallen garbage cans littered the street. Her patio tables lay hidden beneath a mound of branches.

"At least it's not one of the windows," he said, studying the broken doors. "I can have those patched in fifteen minutes."

"Really?"

"You bet. No problem."

Glass crunched under her feet as she took a closer look. Yes, she was lucky it hadn't been one of the huge windows.

He stepped in front of her as he unhooked the string of keys from his belt loop. Cal took a few measurements with the little tape measure attached to his keyring, then snapped it back in place.

"Tell you what. I'll take Ridley home, providing there's not a tree laying on top of my car out front. I've got some left-over ply board in my garage. I'll hook up the generator if the power's out there, too, make a few cuts, then be back here within the hour to cover those up."

They walked into the back room again so she could let him out into the alley. In his absence, she swept up as much glass as she could while musing about the turn of events.

She regretted bringing up how she'd noticed women flocking to him when he brought his fosters. Now it seemed petty and none of her business. While Cal was one of her most frequent customers and she found him hard to ignore in the looks department, his thirst for attention reminded her so much of her ex. The similarity was so off-putting, she struggled to see past her own issue and look at Cal through an objective lens.

Good on his word, Cal reappeared fifty minutes later.

Ginger swept more glass while he worked on the doors. It didn't take him long at all to fit the boards in place and seal everything with duct tape. She leaned the broom against the counter and came over to inspect his handiwork when he finished.

"You've gone above and beyond, Cal. I mean it."

"It helps that my dad is a contractor. I used to work for him when I was younger."

She nodded. "It paid off. Thank you. What do I owe you?"

Cal waved away her question. "Don't worry about it."

"Seriously? Thank you."

"Let me know if you need anything else." He dug his wallet from his back pocket and handed over a business card. "In case something comes up."

She read it to herself, smiling.

Sunrise Solutions
Integrated Business Management Software
Cal Donner, Owner

She had no idea what he did when he wasn't lounging on Coffee Loft's patio, showing off his latest four-legged friend, but this surprised her. He seemed so...not serious enough to be in the computer business.

"What's so funny?" he asked.

"Nothing really... Well, I just realized that after all the times you've come in, I had no idea what you did." She lifted a shoulder.

"It pays the bills. And working from home, I'm able to tend to whomever's keeping my feet warm at the moment."

Confused, she looked at him sharply.

"I'm talking about the dogs, not women," he said with a one-sided grin.

"Of course." She tucked his card in her skirt pocket.

"I have a dog bed under my desk." He cocked his head, squinting at her. "You don't have a very favorable impression of me, do you?"

"After what you did for me here tonight? That's not true at all." She crossed her arms and looked at him squarely while her pulse hammered in her head. This was getting personal.

He rocked back on his heels with a self-satisfied smirk.

"Favorable enough that you'll forgive Ridley and me for getting into your personal space?" He chuckled.

The shower. She'd never forget that.

"You're forgiven. I mean, you're kind of a hero tonight. Who else would have sealed up the doors for me so quickly?"

She almost slapped a hand against her forehead when she noted the look on his face. The word "hero" apparently inflated him like a helium balloon. She should have left it alone after complimenting him the first time.

You always take compliments a step too far.

Now Cal probably thought she was coming on to him.

She loved getting praise—it was her love language after all—and figured everyone else did, too. But if Cal puffed out his chest any more, he'd float away. Some people took her compliments the wrong way, especially men. As if her niceties were a hint that she wanted something. But after the wicked storm, she was almost giddy with relief that her shop withstood the onslaught of wind and rain.

"It's late, and I'm sure you have better places to be. I'll lock the door behind you, then I'm going to head upstairs."

He nodded with a faraway look in his eyes, but he didn't move.

"Good night?" She moved toward the door.

Cal jumped as if she'd jostled him out of a daydream. "Right! I'm going."

"Thanks again, Cal."

"Anytime. If anything else comes up, let me know." He paused with his hand on the door. "Maybe I should get your number. I could call tomorrow, see if you thought of anything more that I could do." There was that look again, the one that was one part hope and the other part smarmy confidence.

"You're in here enough that I'll just catch you when I see you. If I need anything." There. He couldn't read too much into that.

"You're right. Don't hesitate." He pushed open the door. "Have a good night."

Ginger watched him pass by the window and out of sight.

She'd have to make it up to him somehow. He'd done her a huge favor. But repaying him while keeping her distance was the trick.

4

I'm not sure what won my heart first, that adorable mug wall next to the counter or the hand drawn artsy menu board, but the creamy goodness of the café au lait sealed the deal. ~ Customer 4 Life

Two days later, he still basked in the glow of Ginger's compliment.

You're kind of a hero tonight.

Her words had played in his head like the sweetest melody all weekend long. He'd gone to bed early that night after the storm just so he could fall asleep with her voice still fresh in his memory.

I'm her hero.

He shook his head at the thought. That's not what she meant. There's a big distinction between "a" hero and "her" hero. Still, he could dream.

Get real, you sap. There's never been the slightest hint

23

that she was interested. Maybe an occasional stare when he glanced her way, but he attributed that to keeping an eye on his dogs who loved an attentive audience. Sometimes they got a little enthusiastic.

Cal headed down the sidewalk toward Coffee Loft's patio for his midday break. Wispy cotton clouds drifted across an autumn sky of robin's-egg blue, a stark contrast from the other night. Sticks and leaves still littered the sidewalk, but most of the debris had already been cleared by Greenhaven's city workers. He'd heard that a microburst had caused much of the damage in the downtown area, not an actual tornado. He counted Greenhaven as lucky since some of the surrounding towns had experienced more severe weather.

He claimed his usual table in the far corner of the patio so he could watch people coming and going along the sidewalk. His newest foster, Lola, looked up as if wondering why they'd stopped walking. He scooped her up and settled her in his lap. Inside, Ginger's faint outline bustled into the lobby to serve drinks. His pulse stuttered with the tiniest glimpse of her.

Ever since the day almost two years ago that he'd stopped at Coffee Loft's walk-up window on his way home from the park, his visits had become as regular as the chiming in St. Anne's bell tower down the block. The quirky vibe, the hometown friendliness, and the oversized patio, shaded underneath two overarching redbud trees, called his name.

And Ginger had caught his attention instantly when she delivered his drink to the table on that first day. The Lab mix he'd fostered at the time thought Ginger was stopping by to say hello. He'd come out from under the table where he'd parked himself, hitting the underside of the table with his immense head, and upended the hot drink across the surface and onto the front of Cal's shirt and pants. It was hard to say who'd been more horrified, Ginger or him. He'd scored a profuse apology and a twenty-dollar gift card, but that was kibble compared to the heady mix of sharp-witted banter that followed. She was graciously apologetic, even though the fault lay squarely on him for bringing the dog.

His first impression came by way of her perfume, a scent he could only describe as Instant-Crush-in-a-Bottle. Her dark-haired beauty entranced him, but what he admired most was her commanding presence. Coffee Loft hummed along day and night like a bustling, stream-lined machine, thanks to her. As a business owner himself, he knew the dedication and drive it took to keep things running. She was always there, working the counter, cleaning tables, and greeting customers like they were family, with a ready smile and engaging chatter.

Despite the promise of their first encounter, coffee-soaked clothes aside, it'd become clear that Ginger wasn't interested in anything more than a hey-how-are-you-thanks-for-coming-in-have-a-nice-day kind of relationship. She was all business. And that made her all the more appealing. Call it a sweet challenge, or part of his business acumen of troubleshooting software problems, but her disinterest spurred him on. He was a likable guy, he'd been told. How could she resist?

But despite wishing for more, he lay low. The possibility of jeopardizing their coffee-fueled relationship stopped him from making a move. That, and plain ol' nerves. He could chat up a storm in casual settings, but anything romance-wise, he wasn't so smooth.

Lola settled at his feet when he set her down again to answer an e-mail on his phone. He'd almost finished replying when a pair of strappy black sandals appeared near his feet. Toes painted amber, with a heart outlined in tiny clear gemstones on each big toenail, made him smile. He looked up.

"Ridley has shrunk," said Ginger, glancing down at the corgi-bassett mix.

Cal laughed. "Ridley's taking it easy on his dog bed at home. I'm acclimating Lola to my favorite hangout."

"You have two fosters now?"

"I've had as many as five at a time. I wouldn't repeat that again unless someone was desperate."

"Aren't they *all* desperate?"

Cal glanced at her, trying to gauge if she was sincere, but she gazed back at him with a neutral expression. Her green eyes shone brighter in the afternoon light. If only there was a polite way to stare.

"Yes, you're right. But Lola was found cowering behind a dumpster during a thunderstorm. That counts as an emergency."

"Oh, that poor little thing."

Ginger pressed a hand to her heart and gazed at Lola with knitted brows. She didn't reach down to pet her, even as Lola took a tentative step forward to sniff her shoe. But Ginger appeared to be thinking heavy thoughts, judging by her fixed look.

"If you're looking for a new furry friend, Lola's a gem. She's the perfect lady except for a bizarre aversion to squeaky toys." He wouldn't mention that Lola cowered at the sound, piddling wherever she stood without discretion. "And her adoption fee is only one hundred seventy-five."

That snapped Ginger back to the present. "Oh, gosh no. I don't have time for a dog."

"And...there's the cat thing, right?"

"Yes, that." Ginger's shoulders settled as she looked at him. "What can I get you today?"

His usual was a café au lait. He was a creature of habit who rarely wavered, but Ginger asked anyway. It offered the right amount of kick without the bitterness of straight coffee or the sweetness of the sugary drinks. But for some reason, change was on the menu today.

"Iced vanilla latte today, half sweet, please."

"Feeling adventurous, I see." Ginger's smile told him she liked this idea.

"It's a nod to Lola. We found out she was pregnant when we brought her into the shelter. She had three pups who have already been adopted. They were the Coffee Crew. She's Lola Latte. Her pups were Mocha, Brew, and Frappe."

"That's adorable." Again, she paused and looked down at Lola like something else was on her mind. Did she need him for something and was afraid to ask? He'd made it clear he was happy to help. Maybe he should remind her the offer still stood.

"I'll get that latte for you right away." Ginger disappeared back inside before he could speak up. Another missed opportunity. Story of his life.

While he waited, he let Lola wander to the end of her leash. The dog zigzagged on a scent trail, ending at a chair occupied by a woman reading a book with her back to Cal. Lola sat and looked up expectantly at the woman as if she held a treat.

"Well, hello there," the woman said as she glanced down, reaching to scratch Lola's neck.

Lola responded by putting two front paws on the woman's chair. Her hind end wiggled.

Cal got up to get Lola away from the woman. The dog was still getting used to her leash, so Cal hesitated to tug on it at all. He scooped her up in one arm.

"Sorry to bother you," he said.

The woman closed her book and turned to look up at him. "No bother at all. What a sweetie."

"This is Lola."

Lola squirmed so much to get close to the woman that Cal had to set her down again lest she fall out of his arms. Lola promptly scurried up to rest her paws on the woman's lap again.

"She's a little short on manners, but we're working on them." He tried to gently pull Lola away, but the woman protested.

"Really, it's okay. I love dogs." She tucked her hair behind one ear and smiled.

"I never know how much is too much. Not everyone likes dogs." Cal tried to ignore the fact that the woman's gaze hadn't left his face since he apologized. "But she's on a mission to make friends wherever she goes."

"How old is she?" The woman finally broke her gaze to ruffle Lola's back.

"We think she's around three years old."

"We?" She looked boldly at his left hand as he stood there with his thumb hooked into his front pocket.

"The staff at Hearts Fur Love Rescue. Lola is my foster dog."

She got all melty like women usually did when he told them he volunteered at a rescue.

"That's ah-mazing! Bless you for doing that!" Her voice rose an octave with overdone enthusiasm. She was definitely flirting with him.

Ginger cleared her throat at the same time he heard the ice cubes in his drink rattle behind him. He caught her frown before Ginger turned it right side up when she looked at him.

"Here you go. Enjoy," she said.

"Thank you." He led Lola away from her new best friend to follow Ginger. Now was the time to ask before she got away again.

"Hey, Ginger?"

She'd hurried across the patio so quickly he'd almost missed his chance. With her hand on the door handle, she stopped. "Yes?"

He nodded to the doors. "They look good. You got them replaced quicker than I thought you would."

"The window company guys came this morning." Ginger let go of the door. Her fingers wandered to the chain around her neck where she toyed with the silver 'G.' "I was a bit surprised myself since there were so many boarded up doors and windows downtown."

"So...do you need me to do anything else?" He rubbed his chin, a nervous habit. She'd always made him a little self-conscious. Something about her eyes, freezing him in place when she looked his way. He was helpless when she did that.

His question seemed to soften her a bit. Her gaze flickered over him, resting on Lola at his feet. The little dog wiggled when she noticed she had an audience again. This was perfect. Lola had turned into a regular social butterfly right before his eyes this last hour. A socialized dog was an adoptable dog.

"I don't think so."

"Okay, well, if you change your mind."

Ginger knelt down and held out her hand to Lola. The dog licked Ginger's fingers, which brought a smile.

"Actually, there might be something. But I have to get back inside since Jace called in today. I'll reach out soon, okay?"

"You bet." *Keep it casual, keep it cool.*

Ginger's fingers fell away from her necklace as she stood. "Perfect. I'll be in touch."

As she left him standing on the patio, he stood transfixed by the way her ponytail danced across her back when she opened the door. Faint notes of her perfume carried toward him on the breeze. *Vanilla and...something floral?*

He rubbed his jaw. The condensation from the iced drink dampened his skin. The iced *vanilla* drink.

Idiot.

Lola nudged his leg as if to confirm that sentiment.

"Don't even tell me that I'm mistaking the patchouli oil I

massaged into you earlier for a ladies' perfume," he whispered.

Lola's ears perked, and she whined.

Across the patio, the woman who'd flirted with him earlier wore a hopeful expression. He took that as a sign that he should leave.

She'd be in touch, Ginger had said.

And I'll be holding my breath until then.

5

"*Coffee Loft in Greenhaven is a really unique space. The patio is perfect for sipping, people watching, and/or working. This gem of a place even had adoptable dogs on the day I visited. How cool is that?*" ~ Coffee Fan

Later that night, Ginger tucked her feet underneath her as she sank into the couch after cleaning up from dinner. Her good friend Kit Wendell had finally found a free day from ferrying clients up and down the river on her charter boat. Kit lived in Port Chance, one of the historic river towns along this stretch of the Mississippi.

"You weren't on the water when that storm came through, were you? Wasn't it awful?" Ginger sipped the iced ginger peach tea she'd poured for them after dinner. Beside her, Daisy's purring vibrated against her hip. The cat curled into a tight ball which signaled she'd sleep the rest of the night away.

"It was a close call." Kit's eyes popped. "I'd just docked with a group celebrating an eighty-year-old's birthday. The wind sent one poor lady's umbrella into the trees. I had to help half of them to their cars so they wouldn't get blown into the shrubs."

"What a nightmare if you had still been on the water. It was bad enough in the shop."

"I know." She took her iced tea from where Ginger set it on the end table. "Thank goodness there wasn't more damage downstairs than the broken door panes," Kit said. She inspected the green hobnail glass after she sampled the tea. "This is yummy, by the way."

"Thanks. I'm testing a new brand for the shop. I think it's a winner."

"I'll second that." Kit set the glass on the coaster again, then settled back into the wing chair. "So, tell me more about the guy who helped with the repairs. What's his story?"

"Not much of a story. He's a regular. Brings his foster dogs onto the patio most of the time." She wrinkled her nose.

"You're lucky he came in that night."

She nodded. "I am. I offered to pay him, but he wouldn't take anything."

Kit wound the end of her long braid around her finger. "The way you talked about him, it sounded like there's a little more to your history together."

Ginger looked at her lap and smoothed the wrinkles in her shirt. "Not much to tell."

Kit snickered. "Are you sure about that?"

"Why wouldn't I be?"

"Why? Because I've never seen you brush off a topic faster than you did when I asked about him the first time."

She looked out the front window. Had she avoided talking about Cal? It wasn't intentional. Maybe Kit's question had caught her off guard is all.

"You haven't dated in a while." Kit asked with a wry smile. "Is this one on your radar?"

That's what she liked about Kit. She didn't hold back—in her opinions, questions, or life in general. She'd met her when Kit stopped in Coffee Loft a year ago last summer with her oldest sister Rose to drop off a batch of cider donuts from Rose's bakery at Apple Hill Farm. Rose recommended Coffee Loft as a supplier for Kit's morning boat tour package. During Kit's subsequent twice-monthly visits to Coffee Loft, she and Kit had become good friends. There wasn't anything Kit couldn't do, be it changing out a bathroom faucet, replacing a car battery, or—as she'd experienced first-hand—patching a leaky spot on the roof near the building's chimney. But date Cal? Obviously, Kit lacked matchmaking skills. She couldn't be more wrong.

"Nope. I'm taking a break."

Kit snorted. "It's been a long break if I'm remembering right. But I'd be a hypocrite if I tried to sell you on the merits of dating. What's changed?"

"It's exhausting. The small talk, the pretense. I'm not that great at first impressions."

"You're the face of Coffee Loft. Everyone loves you."

"Running a business is a lot different than dating."

"Nah. It's all public relations. At least, initially." Kit shrugged.

"That's what I have trouble with, the transition period."

"That only means you haven't found the right guy."

"I'm beginning to think there isn't anyone else out there for me."

She took another sip of tea to hide her frown. Since her divorce, she'd opened Coffee Loft and relished the freedom of steering her life in whatever direction she pleased. But sometimes she missed the companionship. The shared dreams. The *possibilities*. Early in her marriage, she'd had all that with Marco. But then suddenly she didn't when he decided someone else's company was more preferable than hers. The drama happened long ago, though, and she'd moved on. Bitterness had dissolved over the years as she focused more on herself. Still, the trust issues remained.

Kit looped her arms around her bent knees. "I'd just get up and leave if there was no connection."

She chuckled at Kit's candidness. "I wish I could do that. I'm more of the suffer-in-silence type."

Kit let out an exasperated sigh. "So, back to the door-fixer guy. Maybe he came to your rescue for a reason."

"What's that supposed to mean?"

"I bet he wouldn't have done that for just anyone." Kit pointed at her. "Maybe it's a sign that you should ask him out."

"*What?* I think not."

"But you have so much in common."

She laughed at the ridiculousness of it as a buzz tickled

its way up her spine at the same time. Her and Cal Donner... together...on a *date?*

"What are you basing that on, the fact that he comes in for coffee?"

"I'm sure many solid relationships have been built over cold brews."

"He's so outgoing. I'm a complete introvert. And he's a software consultant. What does that even mean? I'm feeling lucky if the computer doesn't crash at least once a day."

Kit laughed. "You're both business owners. And you like pets."

"Hey, Kit?" She held a hand to her mouth for the stage whisper. "Stick to steering boats. You're a terrible match-maker. The guy has multiple dogs at a time. My only experience with dogs is offering a fresh bowl of water to the ones he brings here."

"It's a starting point."

"Or a point of no return."

"Fine." Kit frowned.

She finished off her tea and rolled an ice cube around in her mouth. "But I have been thinking of reaching out to him..."

Kit smacked her hands together, excited. "See? Now we're talking."

"No, not like that. I've been mulling over the idea of asking him for a testimonial. It's for the portfolio I'm supposed to submit because of my Forty Professionals Under Forty nomination."

"You could literally choose any one of your other fifty

thousand customers." Kit gave her a wink. "This is just an excuse to get close to him."

"Wrong. The constant parade of dogs on my patio is a little much, but I'm trying to be objective here. Most of the customers seem to love him and his dogs when he brings one by. Everyone gravitates toward him."

"Except you."

She ignored the comment. "I'm supposed to highlight someone who has been positively impacted by me or my business. His dogs have, I'm sure. I know of at least one family that adopted through the shelter because they met Cal on the patio."

"Exactly!" Kit nodded.

She slumped, giving Kit a look. "You're just humoring me now."

"Guilty." She grinned. "Okay, in all seriousness, just call him."

"You think?"

Kit nodded again.

"What do I have to lose, right?"

The conversation turned to Kit's busy schedule for Muddy Bottom Tours, her sister Janie's upcoming wedding, and plans for the neighborhood fall festival. Kit offered to help set up for the day if Ginger thought more hands were needed.

When Kit left a short time later, Ginger beelined it for her bag resting on one of the bar stools at the kitchen counter. When she couldn't find Cal's business card in her wallet, she remembered sticking it in the desk drawer in her office downstairs. Merris had closed the store an hour ago, so Ginger hurried down to Coffee Loft to find the card and call Cal from there.

The shop was dark and quiet, and the scent of roasted beans calmed her taut nerves. She swallowed against the tightness in her throat, slipped Cal's business card from the desk drawer, and tapped his number into her phone. The seconds between hitting the last number and the call connecting were punctuated by her heartbeat thudding in her head.

Why is this such a big deal?

Cal answered before she thought about how to answer that.

"Hello?"

"Hi, Cal. It's Ginger."

"It's late. Is something wrong?" His tone was off, like she'd caught him at a bad time.

"Not at all. I just have something to ask you, and it's perfectly fine if you say no."

Silence.

Maybe warming him up a little instead of jumping right into her reason for calling would have been a better idea. Or maybe she shouldn't have called at all.

What if he was on a date? The possibility heated her face.

Just ask him.

"I'm wondering if you'd give me a testimonial." *There. That wasn't so bad.*

More silence.

"Hello?"

39

"What for?" he asked. In the background, metal clanged like he was rearranging pots and pans. "Hold on."

The noise grew muffled as if he'd covered the phone with his hand. Seconds passed. Ginger took a deep breath. It was a big ask, she knew. He'd already fixed her doors for free, and now this. She didn't want to give him the impression that she was all take and no give. What could she do for him?

"Okay, I'm back," he said. "Why on earth do you want to interview *me*?"

She gritted her teeth. *Here goes.*

"I've been nominated for that Forty Under Forty Award. You know the one that—"

"Oh, right. The movers and shakers of the Quad Cities," he said. "What a huge honor. Congratulations," he said, distractedly. In the background, a dog yipped. Something crashed before a door slammed.

"Did I catch you in the middle of something? I can call back at another time." Talking to her was probably the last thing he wanted to be doing right now. It was late. It sounded like he was busy. *And why is it so hot in here?* She glanced at the thermostat on the wall while fanning her face with her free hand. Had she accidentally turned the heat on today? She tugged at the neck of her tee-shirt. Her hair felt like it was on fire.

"No...no, not at all," he said, out of breath.

"Anyway, I have to submit a portfolio. A résumé, personal statement, references. That sort of thing." It was definitely a mistake, calling him.

"Uh huh." There was a smugness in his tone. "I'm not sure where I fit into all of that."

"I want to interview you for a little profile I want to write. You know, a feel-good story. About one of my most interesting customers." He's going to see right through that heap of hooey. She shuffled through the application papers until she came to the portfolio requirements. "It says, 'Submit a five-hundred-word profile on a co-worker, business associate, or customer who has been positively impacted by you and/or the business you work for, along with a fifty-word testimonial from that person.'"

When he didn't say anything, Ginger held her phone out to see if they were still connected.

"That's intense," he said.

"It is."

Cal let out a little sigh. "I'll have to think about it," he said nonchalantly.

She blinked. Of all the ways for him to respond, she didn't expect a noncommittal answer.

"Okay, then take your time." She let out an awkward laugh. "And, no worries if you decide it's a bad idea. I have someone else waiting in the wings." She totally didn't.

"Good to know that you have a back-up plan. In case, you know, I decide to decline."

"You bet." Ginger clenched a hand and tapped her fist against her forehead.

"I'll let you know tomorrow," he said. "Thanks for thinking of me."

She looked at her phone as their call disconnected. Now would be the perfect time to go to bed and pull the covers over her head until next year.

She stalked over to the refrigerator, looking for something

to take her mind off of how she'd just made a complete fool of herself. Thank goodness he was clueless about the butterflies in her stomach, beating against her ribcage as she talked with him. She opened the door, staring blankly at the contents, her thoughts tumbling over one another to make sense of Cal's answer.

He'd *think* about it?

What was so complicated about her request? A simple "yes" or "no" would have worked just fine. And why was she stewing about this?

The refrigerated air fanned the heat of embarrassment as she replayed the conversation again in her mind. Was he playing games? Why would he do that?

What she knew about Cal Donner could be summed up in one word: intentional. Cal wasn't the wishy-washy sort. He knew what to order the second he stepped up to the counter. He didn't hesitate when he offered to fix her doors. He had never adopted one of his fosters, though he'd been tempted in the past, he claimed. *I can do more good fostering many than owning a couple.* And he'd certainly never said, *I'll think about it* before.

She eyed the can of whipped topping, popped the lid off, and dispensed a cloud of cream into her mouth. The sweetness melted on her tongue as she looked at the almost-empty can in her hand, her thoughts still far away.

Of course, he'd picked a fine time to be indecisive with her portfolio deadline coming up. She almost wished she hadn't been nominated for the award now that she'd told Cal about it. The only other people who knew were Kit and the person that nominated her, Josie Runyon, another loyal customer. Unfortunately, Josie was a self-proclaimed recluse who'd decline on the spot if Ginger asked to interview her instead.

In the stillness of the shop, Ginger groaned out loud. She squirted one more generous helping from the canister into her mouth, then tossed it in the garbage.

Whereas she was all out of whipped cream, there was plenty of Cal-fueled angst to go around.

6

Coffee Loft's café au laits—primo! ~ #1 Fan

Lola and Ridley lounged on the day bed together, keeping an eye on Cal as he collapsed in his office chair. The little dog nestled snugly under the bigger dog's neck like a puzzle piece. They'd finally settled down after Cal discovered a mouse in one of his kitchen cabinets. It ran for its little life before disappearing under the door to his basement. The dogs' pursuit ended with them crashing into the basement door, almost sweeping him off his feet while he unloaded the dishwasher. A stainless-steel bowl and a handful of silverware were the only casualties that hit the floor. Figures that Ginger had called in the middle of the chaos.

"She wants to interview me, guys. What do you think of that?"

Ridley twitched his tail before closing his eyes and drifting sideways onto the mattress. Lola was a bit more receptive to the idea. One ear flicked up as she cocked her head, her trademark pose.

"I know, right? That means she thinks I'm *interesting*."

At that, Lola yawned.

Positively impacted, huh?

"Have I been positively impacted by Coffee Loft?" He kicked his feet up onto the daybed to think about that for a minute. Lola sniffed his socks, then gave him one of her doggy smiles.

Ginger played a large part in why Coffee Loft was his go-to destination with the dogs. She was very accommodating in letting him bring his dogs there. Not many places would appreciate furry patrons, even if they were confined to the patio. Ginger's generosity had indirectly helped some of the dogs from Hearts Fur Love Rescue get adopted. He knew for a fact that people he'd met outside Coffee Loft had later come in to the shelter and, ultimately, adopted dogs into their forever homes.

Cal twirled around in his chair, facing his monitor. He'd been in the middle of wrapping up a project shortly before Ginger called. Now there was maybe a one-in-a-million chance of finishing tonight since his brain buzzed with possibilities.

I'll let you know. That's what he'd told her.

But even as he uttered the words, he had no idea what he'd meant. What *was* his game plan?

He tapped his fingers on the keyboard.

If there was a way to prolong this interview, turn it into a longer time commitment, he just might crack open that professional exterior she wore so perfectly.

But how?

He leaned back, hooking his hands behind his head, and stared at the ceiling. The elaborate chandelier above winked at him, reminding him once again he needed to change it out for a more practical ceiling fan. Whoever owned the house before he bought it had used this room for a dining room. The little table overlooking the back patio suited him just fine for eating. His lifestyle was far from needing a fancy and formal dining space with a glass chandelier.

Fancy. Formal. Chandeliers.

An idea was coming to light.

Dogs...lots of dogs...

"Yes—that's it!"

Lola and Ridley let out a bark.

He sat upright and scanned his messy office. So many piles. Where could it be?

The bright green postcard peeking out from underneath the ink cartridge box caught his eye seconds later. He grabbed it, smiling as he reviewed the details:

The Rhinestones and Rawhides Gala

October 30th. Doors open at 5 p.m. for cocktails.

Century Ballroom, Addler Hotel, Bedden

Enjoy a pawsitively fun night out on the town to support our efforts in helping dogs find their furever homes.

He waved the postcard in the air like a victory flag.

"A gala! How will she say no to this, guys?" But, behind

him, the couch was empty. His captive audience had left the room at some point while he was busy patting himself on the back.

He studied the postcard again. The annual fundraiser came with new urgency this year. The city had announced a new sewer project which would encompass part of the shelter's property. To no avail, Charleen, the Hearts Fur Love director, had sat through many a planning meeting trying to make a case to not involve the shelter. The shelter's board members were now on the hunt to find new facilities before the end of the year.

The shelter's plight would be the perfect selling point to get Ginger to join him at the gala.

"She won't turn me down once I make my case," he whispered to himself. "Not if she wants that interview."

7

"Completely obsessed with this place. Every time I'm in the neighborhood I have to stop. Coffee is wonderful, the ambience is a close second. Love Coffee Loft!" ~ Chai M.

Ginger wasn't much of a runner, but she liked to think she was. It was fall mornings like this, when she rose while the sun still hid below the horizon, that she thought about getting serious. It'd been way too long since her last run.

On her balcony, the birds chittered as they dug into the sunflower seeds, peanuts, and cracked-corn mix on the feeders. A fall tapestry of leaves littered her mosaic table and chairs. Soon she'd have to fold them into the tiny closet just outside the back door when it turned too cold to eat breakfast on the balcony.

The cool tinge of autumn air made her second-guess the

decision of not grabbing a jacket as she ventured downstairs to fast-walk the three blocks to the park. There, she'd run twelve laps—three miles, no less, no more—around the gravel path circling the park's perimeter. A few joggers were already out, huffing along the route when she joined them. She adjusted her earbuds as she started slowly, dodging a woman walking her four-legged fluffball who seemed oblivious to anyone else.

She thought about the day's to-do list as her feet slapped a rhythmic tempo on the path.

Place Christmas merchandise order.

Decide on holiday drink menu.

Interview two people for seasonal work.

Planning the fall festival was a list all by itself. It'd be here before she knew it, and she'd barely come up with an agenda.

Finish Forty Under Forty portfolio.

Cal.

No matter what she did lately, he managed to wiggle his way into her thoughts. The storm throwing them together was to blame for that. When she lay awake last night stewing about how he'd put off answering her about the interview, she'd tried putting her finger on what had changed. At one-thirty in the morning, she finally came up with an answer: no one had ever made her feel so cared for as he did that night.

He'd stepped up in an instant to help her in a crisis, no strings attached, and it had overwhelmed her with gratitude. There was a psychology term for that, wasn't there? White Knight Syndrome or something to do with falling in love with a person who rescues you?

Except I am not in love with Cal Donner.

She turned up the volume of the music, hoping to push the thoughts back where they belonged—in the quiet, dark recesses of her mind. The place where all annoyances went to die.

Three laps into her run, she was barely winded and feeling pretty proud of herself. She glanced far ahead on the path to where a group milled around the park's kiosk with their dogs. She slowed, squinting against the bright sunlight, searching for one dog walker in particular. Not that she *wanted* to see him, but hoped to avoid him. Of course, that was it.

But there was no mistaking Cal's dark hair and broad shoulders. Or Ridley the horse-dog on one leash and Lola on the other.

Turn around before he spots you.

Too late. Cal zeroed in on her almost as if she'd shouted his name. He waved heartily.

As he came toward her on the path, grinning like he knew the effect of his leading-man looks, she wanted to hide.

"Ginger! Good morning."

Her teeny, tiny running shorts and her barely there polypropylene tank didn't cover nearly enough. Worse was the way Cal's gaze swept over her like he hadn't had breakfast and she was the tastiest-looking pastry in the history of fresh-baked goods.

Goosebumps ran rampant up her arms like an army of mice.

It'd been ages since she noticed a man look at her like that. And she kind of liked the way he cocked his head to the side with laser-focused admiration, and maybe like he was trying to figure her out at the same time.

"I didn't know you were a runner," he said, tightening the dogs' leashes around his hand before they bound her legs together with their frenzied circling. "I've never seen you here."

That's because I can't commit. "Maybe we just miss each other," she said. Inwardly, she cringed at stretching the truth.

He shrugged. "It's hard to pay attention to anything else when I'm surrounded by that crew." He nodded over his shoulder at the chaotic mix of dogs and their walkers, and she took the opportunity to yank the legs of her shorts down for more coverage.

"I can imagine." A little upward tug on her tank's neckline wouldn't hurt either.

"It's a nice morning, eh?" He turned back to her just as she planted her hands on her hips again.

She wished he'd return to his group so she could run back to her place, change into something less revealing, and pretend this encounter never happened.

"Beautiful. Listen, I—"

"I've decided to adopt him." He nodded to Ridley.

"Yeah?"

He nodded. "Lola might be going to her forever home in a few days, and poor Ridley follows her around like she's the apple of his eye."

"What's the name for that, a bonded pair? Maybe they should be adopted together." When she looked down at Lola, the little dog raised her paw. "Why is she doing that?"

"She's trying to appeal to your sympathy. This is one clever dog, let me tell you."

"So you're going to give Ridley a home because you feel sorry for him?"

"That's about right."

"I thought you told me you don't adopt, just foster?"

"You changed my mind."

"I did?" She didn't remember having that conversation.

"You said you don't have time for a dog." He shrugged. "I do, since I work from home. I just felt selfish, spreading myself around to all of these dogs and not committing to any of them long-term."

Did he just indirectly tell her she's selfish? Or was that her own guilt talking?

"I really need to get going—"

"Wait."

Ginger walked in a tight circle. Her pulse was slowing. She'd never make it back to shower and open the store on time—

"Yes, I'll do the interview."

She stopped. "Really? That's great." All that worrying for nothing. Of course, he'd do the interview. This was Cal, Doer of Good Deeds and White Knight Storm Rescuer.

"On one condition."

"Like I said, anything." She shook out her legs, keeping her muscles warm, and waited.

He slipped something from his back pocket and handed it over. "I was going to stick this in your mailbox on the way past the shop this morning."

She stopped moving. "What is it?" She turned the post-card over, then turned it over again.

"An invite to the shelter's annual fundraiser. If you want to interview me, you'll have to come."

A fizzy sensation coiled underneath her ribcage, making it momentarily hard to breathe.

"Can't I just send some money? I probably won't know anyone." Her face heated when she realized her obvious misstep. "Except you, of course."

"I'm sure you'll recognize more people than you think." That over-eager expression lit his face again. It really brightened his blue eyes.

She looked at the postcard again. "It's formal, too?"

"Time to go shopping." Cal crossed his arms, leaning against a stone water fountain. His look was completely uncompromising. There was even a little smirk twitching his lips, like he was thinking, *I've got her now.*

Not having a dress was a sorry excuse for turning down an invitation, but she wasn't thinking straight. Her mind whirled with images of them in formalwear, sneaking glances at each other all night with awkward regularity. Having to make small talk. And the only dress she owned that wasn't a sundress or a beach cover-up was a dreadful teal thing with balloon sleeves she'd worn as a bridesmaid ten years ago. She'd hated it at the time, too, since it overwhelmed her slight frame. *Why is it even still in my closet?*

"So what do you say?" Cal picked up Lola who'd started tugging on her leash to get back to the other dogs. "I'll give you the interview you want if you come as my date to the fundraiser."

Her focus snapped back to him. *Date?*

Cal smiled. "Don't worry. It'll be a one-and-done date. Kind of like a blind date that you know won't work out beforehand."

"It's not a blind date. I know you."

He ticked off another argument by raising a finger. "But not as well as you think."

"Right."

"Hence the interview."

She lifted her chin, looking squarely at him. "It's a big ask for twenty minutes of your time."

She joked, but the turmoil happening in her stomach at the moment didn't lie. And what was the little tickle in the back of her throat? Seasonal allergies? No. Did she swallow a bug? Nope. She put a hand against her neck, trying to rub it away.

"Not such a big ask if I help you get that top spot on the Forty Under Forty list," he said.

He is so right.

Resigned, she nodded. "It's a deal."

He extended his hand. The tiny grin had turned into a full-blown smile. "Shake on it."

That odd sensation in her middle rippled when she slipped her hand into his. The gentle warmth of his grip surprised her.

Their eyes locked for a few extra seconds and her mouth went dry.

What is happening?

Lola must have sensed some important decision had just been made because she lurched in Cal's arms toward her.

Ginger caught Lola's front half to keep her from falling to the ground. Lola took full advantage of the situation by lapping at Ginger's chin.

"Dog kisses are the best, aren't they?" Cal asked, chuckling. He wasn't even trying to pull her back.

"Nothing better," she said while holding her breath. *A fluoride rinse would do wonders for these dogs' adoption appeal.* It was so hard to keep smiling with this dog kissing her. To make matters worse, her pointy little tongue kept darting up Ginger's nose.

Cal positively beamed. His captivating eye wrinkles were at their finest. *At least there is that.*

"I'm going to get back to the group and let you continue your run. Let me know when a good time is for that interview." He winked.

She stood rooted to the spot as he walked away. Her brain felt like someone had pushed the pulse speed on a blender. Wouldn't Kit love to hear about this turn of events. One of her I-told-you-so comments was imminent if she found out Cal proposed this ridiculous idea.

Yes, the word "date" took his proposal to a whole new level. It wasn't just a ploy to get her to donate to a cause.

Somehow it seemed more personal.

8

"*Cute, cozy and killer coffee. The time I went they were giving out free samples of the seasonal drinks. I'll definitely be back.*" - Liz W.

A few days later, the morning rush had dwindled to just a few customers at the counter, so Ginger grabbed a towel to wipe down tables. Jace got a head start on making more blueberry and cranberry-walnut muffins, and scones to fill the nearly depleted pastry case. Outside, customers took over almost all of the patio tables. Fridays were always the busiest weekday.

She cleaned the last table, then reorganized the condiment station. Merris exited the kitchen with an armload of clean mugs for the mug wall, so Ginger replaced those, too. In a half hour, a potential new hire was coming in for an interview.

Merris sidled up alongside her in front of the cubbies as Ginger set a mug into the last empty spot.

"I forgot to tell you that Cal came in yesterday," Merris said, pointing to a mug. "He brought this one."

Ginger took down the mug. Printed on it was a photo of a cat lounging in a leather recliner wearing glasses, with the words "Dogs have owners. Cats have staff."

Ginger laughed, studying it. "Did he now?"

"Yep. And there wasn't room on the wall, so I put one away that hasn't moved in months."

"No problem. He's regular enough that he's earned his own cubby, don't you think?"

Merris smiled wryly. "Whatever you say, boss."

Ginger replaced the mug, ignoring Merris's sarcasm.

"Speaking of mugs," Merris said, tipping her chin toward the patio.

Outside, Cal pulled out a chair and sat. He'd brought Ridley this time. Maybe Lola was already making herself at home with her new family.

"Should I go see what he wants?" Merris asked.

Cal leaned over to pull the stainless-steel water bowl next to Ridley. Even from inside the shop, Ginger could see half of the water splashing onto the patio as the dog lapped from the bowl. *Good grief, what a moose.*

"No, thanks. I've got it." She took the mug from its perch again and walked it over to the counter where she started his café au lait.

Aside from the other day, for as long as he'd been visiting Coffee Loft, Cal ordered the same drink. She made his café au lait every time without thinking. When it was busy, it was easy to get lost in the moment, working on autopilot through a rush. But maybe this time she'd put a little more effort into Cal's drink, give it a special touch to show how much she appreciated him agreeing to the interview.

She poured a thin ribbon of frothy milk into the mug, waiting for the foam to rise. When it did, Ginger rummaged through the basket of plastic stencils.

A fern—*too generic*.

A heart—*no!*

Here it is—perfect.

She held the stencil over the foam and sprinkled it with cinnamon from a shaker. A little cat face smiled up at her when she took away the stencil. Suppressing a bubble of laughter, she hurried outside before the image distorted.

Coming up behind him, she set the drink down.

He grinned. "I see you found my mug." He did a double take and peered into the cup at the design she'd added. "Nice touch."

"I thought you'd like that. Nice mug, by the way. Are you softening toward the feline population?"

He pulled a mock frown. "Me? Never."

"It's a nice addition to the mug wall. And so on point. By the way, Daisy has a staff of one."

"Daisy?"

"My cat. I haven't mentioned her before?"

He shook his head. "Only that you liked cats."

"Hmm...okay. Now you know."

His grin grew wider. "Thanks for sharing. You, I'm assuming, are Daisy's assistant."

"I am."

"So, no other...staff members?"

"Just me."

"Sounds like a bit of a tyrant." He inched his chair back so he could look up at her more fully. "Can you sit for a bit?"

She glanced through the window to the front counter. Merris helped the last customer, so she pulled out the chair opposite him to sit. Immediately, Ridley nudged his head onto her lap, coating her skirt in drool. Thank goodness the pattern hid most of it, but she was drenched underneath the fabric. Cal didn't notice.

"Is today a good time for that interview? I can meet you back here when you close," he said as he typed something into his phone before laying it face down on the table.

"Honestly, tomorrow would be better. I'm taking it off. Can you meet over your lunch hour?"

He slicked back his hair with one hand, squinting up at the sky as if thinking about it. Her eyes were drawn to the taut bicep muscle underneath his denim shirt, a muscle so well-defined that the fabric only enhanced its shape. Ginger averted her gaze to something less distracting. Ridley's soulful eyes met hers when she looked down at her lap. *Caught you*, the dog's look seemed to say.

Cal tucked his arm at his side and looked at her again. "That should work. Where?"

"How about the fountain at the mall? There's usually a food truck or two. We could find a bench, grab something to eat."

Cal's eyes lit up. "Sold."

She eyed Ridley. "Maybe you should, ah...come alone. No distractions."

"That shouldn't be a problem." He sipped his drink which left a little foam mustache on his lip.

She pointed to her own mouth. "You have..."

Cal swiped at it with the back of his hand.

"We have napkins for that," she said, slipping the cne she'd brought him out from underneath his mug.

Cal's eyes widened, and he leaned away. Did he honestly think she'd wipe it away herself? She chuckled.

"Don't worry. Unless you're under five, I'll let you wipe your own mouth." She waved the napkin for him to take.

Cal swiped it along his lips. "If I were at home, I'd have let Ridley take care of it."

"Gross."

"He's quite useful when he wants to be." There was an infectious twinkle in his eye.

"Cal Donner?"

Ginger startled. A woman had stopped on the sidewalk on the other side of the wrought-iron railing next to their table.

Cal popped up out of his chair so fast he had to steady it from falling backward. "You're Becca, right? Here, come on around and join us," he said, gesturing to the other end of the patio.

The young woman, dressed like she'd just come from the gym, took him up on his offer. She sashayed over to Cal and stuck out her hand.

"It's so nice to meet you. And this must be Ridley," she said, kneeling next to the dog. "What a cutie," she cooed.

"He's that and more. Can I buy you a coffee?"

She stood and waved away the offer. "I can't do caffeine.

Makes my heart go through the roof." Her giggle was so high-pitched that Ridley's ears flickered.

Join us, he'd said. Clearly, he'd meant him and Ridley, not her. She pushed back from the table, suddenly feeling like a third wheel.

"I'm going to get back to work." A little zing of rejection burned in her chest for no good reason.

Cal and the woman looked at her in unison as if noticing her for the first time. To his credit, Cal quickly regained his bearings.

"Tomorrow then," he said. "Say, eleven thirty at the fountain?"

"See you there." She sounded overly chipper even though she felt just the opposite.

Ginger wandered back inside, straightening chairs and checking the garbage can as she left Cal and the mystery woman alone on the patio. Behind the counter, she sporadically kept an eye on them while she restocked the cups and opened boxes of new flavorings. Every time she caught them laughing, her throat tightened. She poured herself some water to wash away that pesky sensation, one that had no business happening in the first place.

Twenty minutes later, Cal and that woman hugged goodbye as Ginger finished a to-go order. She frowned as she handed over the drink carrier to the office assistant who'd come to pick it up.

"Are you all right?" Merris asked as Ginger turned around and found her employee leaning against the back counter with her arms crossed. "You're awfully quiet."

"Of course. Why wouldn't I be?" She brushed her hands together as if that alone might offer a mental reset.

"I don't know. Maybe the cat mug has something to do with it. Like maybe there isn't room for it on the mug wall after all."

Ginger's attention flickered to the empty cubby where Cal's mug had rested a short time ago. She hesitated before giving Merris a reassuring smile.

"Cal can claim a spot for as long as he likes. He practically lives here."

"But does he only come for the coffee?" Merris asked in a lilting tone while tapping her chin.

"I don't know what else it could be." *Besides meeting people on my patio like it's his office away from home.*

"It's you," Merris said.

She turned away before Merris noticed how the teasing had caused her cheeks to flame. But Merris's reply rang in her ears as Ginger left to go check on Jace's progress with the baking.

It's you.

9

I *love this little coffee shop so much. Their chai teas and loaded lemonades are the best!* ~ Libby A.

Every morning, rain or shine, Cal rolled out of bed at a quarter to six, poured his coffee into a thermos which he'd set on auto brew the night before, and hopped in his car to head to Hearts Fur Love Dog Rescue.

As he pulled into the parking lot the next morning, with the sun just beginning to peek over the tree tops on the horizon, the muffled sound of barking dogs greeted Cal. Gravel crunching underneath car tires always set them off. They knew what it meant: a little taste of freedom.

Each of the dogs under the rescue's care needed to be walked four times a day, beginning with the early shift at six thirty in the morning. Most times every one of the shelter's thirty kennels were filled, but thankfully, there was a robust volunteer staff to walk and feed the dogs, and clean the kennels.

Inside the building, Cal took one of the leashes from the wall rack and walked the length of the first row of kennels, to the next dog waiting to be let out. Several volunteers were already leading dogs down the aisles toward the back door.

He came to a scruffy, black mutt that looked like a mix between a Lab and a terrier. His wavy coat shone underneath the fluorescent lights, the effect from a good bath when he'd come in the other day from animal control. The poor guy had been a mess—matted and filthy. He'd been itching up a storm, too, from the burrs stuck on the underside of his ears.

"Sawyer, you look like a new man."

The dog sat back on his haunches and raised his front feet.

"And a charmer, too."

He opened the kennel door to clip the leash onto Sawyer's collar, then walked him down the aisle. Sawyer's jaunty step and ears pricked forward told Cal that the dog had already grown accustomed to kennel life—a good sign. It was the anxious dogs who cowered in the corners of their kennels and shook with fear that tugged at his heartstrings. Those were the dogs who had trouble getting adopted.

Another volunteer named Kelly was just outside the door when he opened it. The older woman always chose the smallest dogs to walk on account of them being easier to control with her arthritic hands.

"Good morning, Kelly."

"Hi, Cal. I hear our Lola is going home soon. That's great news."

"It's wonderful news. Lola and I did a meet-and-greet a few days ago. Paperwork is filled out, so she's ready to go."

"Good for Lola. I hear she'll have a big fenced-in yard to run around in, too."

"And some teenagers to play with."

Kelly looked down at the little chihuahua on the end of her leash. "I wish they could all have that. My heart breaks a little more each time I come in here."

"But it also keeps you coming back to give these guys a little love, doesn't it?"

She nodded. "It sure does."

It took its toll on some of the new volunteers, witnessing the number of dogs who'd been abandoned and rehomed, or bred for profit in deplorable conditions until the breeding operation was shut down. But instead of feeling over-whelmed by the sheer number who needed help, he'd found satisfaction in knowing he could be a part of the solution.

"I hear we may have to find a new place sooner than previously thought," Kelly said.

"Before December?"

"Charleen went to last night's city council meeting. The company who's been contracted to do the work wants to start with preliminary work this fall."

He gritted his teeth. "That doesn't sound good. Is there a plan?"

"She and the board are talking later today to prepare for the worst."

Sawyer tugged on his leash as a sign his patience had run out. Kelly waved good-bye with a smile.

The dog led him along the dirt path on the wooded grounds of the shelter. It was such a peaceful spot of land that he hated to see it go. Progress wasn't always ideal for all involved.

As he walked, his thoughts turned to his meeting with Ginger later on.

There was no way to prepare answers when he didn't know what kinds of questions she'd ask. He knew how to make a convincing argument for adopting dogs, but this time she'd be asking about *him*. It was the perfect chance to give her an unhurried glimpse into his life. Once she got to know him, really learned who he was, she might give him a chance. So far, their relationship had been defined by caffeinated beverages and dog drool.

The hours dragged between the time he left the shelter and when he headed out of his door again to meet Ginger. The fifteen-minute walk to the outdoor mall in downtown Greenhaven was a pleasant one. Leaves skittered along the sidewalk as he passed homes with tidy lawns in his historic neighborhood. The houses gave way to businesses soon enough, and then to the three square blocks that were closed to vehicles. The circular fountain at one of the intersections was the site for the spring arts fair and the weeknight summer music concerts. Food trucks pulled to the closest possible spots on the intersecting streets to access the crowds. Sometimes he came down here instead of taking a dog to Coffee Loft for a change of scenery, especially when he craved an Italian beef sandwich from Vito's Little Italy food truck or one of the strawberry-basil macarons from La Patisserie's dessert cart.

He spotted Ginger sitting on the concrete ledge surrounding the fountain as soon as he arrived at the end of the block. Beside her, there was a bag and two drinks with straws already poked through the plastic lids.

"You're early," Ginger blurted when he stopped in front of her. She laughed as she gathered her hair in one hand, gave it a twist, then tucked it over her shoulder. "I mean, hi, Cal. Sorry, that was rude. You surprised me."

If he was nervous, she seemed completely unstrung. Her shrill laugh was the first sign. The two sloppy gulps she took of her drink was another. Lemonade dribbled out of her mouth and onto the front of her shirt. She dabbed it away hurriedly.

She wore a denim jacket and a long, printed skirt that competed with the colors of the gold and crimson potted mums nearby. Her hair, usually swept back in a long pony-tail, curled around her shoulders. How would he possibly focus on her questions when he couldn't look at her without his thoughts scattering in the breeze?

"I thought I'd order food before everyone swarmed the trucks for the lunch hour," she said.

"Good thinking."

He sat down and studied her while she opened the bags to sort the food. When she held out two sandwiches, Ginger eyed him. In the midday sun, her green eyes held hues of gold and blue. His pulse thudded like the drum solo in "Wipeout" at the way she stared at him for a beat longer than usual.

"Tell me if I'm wrong, but I pegged you as a turkey cranberry wrap kind of guy," she said. "Either that, or you can have my ham and Swiss wrap with mustard. Sorry, I should have asked beforehand."

"Perfection." He took the turkey wrap and a bag of potato chips she pushed toward him, too.

"Eat first, talk second," she said.

Cal hid a smile behind his sandwich. Ginger's assertiveness might be intimidating to anyone else, but it was a part of her that he found most charming.

They sat in comfortable silence for the first few minutes, eating and watching the noontime crowd. With her initial reaction behind them, Ginger didn't seem the slightest bit self-conscious, unlike him. Could she hear his stomach churning and notice his hand shaking while he sipped his drink?

"I used to come down here for lunch all the time when I first opened the shop," she mused. "Now I'm realizing how much I miss it."

Two guys had stopped at one of the benches on the other side of the fountain and unloaded a saxophone and violin from their respective cases. When they started to play, she smiled. She thumbed toward them.

"And the buskers I miss the most." She looked so serene, practically glowing as the men started to play.

"Why did you stop coming?"

She shrugged. "I got caught up in the idea that if I wasn't at work, it'd fail."

"Impossible."

Ginger gave him a look as if he were wrong. "After that other coffee place opened on Second Avenue—"

"I know the one."

"I thought we were history. The profit margin did dip, and that scared me."

"Then what happened?"

"I stopped dwelling on it." She laughed. "I saw the same faces come back day after day, and I realized they're not drawn to the big brand name. They prefer the little neighborhood place instead. So I played that up even more. Added the mug wall, the drink suggestion board, the little homey touches." She nudged him. "The dog bowl on the patio."

"Hey, not gonna lie. That drew me in."

She laughed. "I'm glad it did."

"I'm, uh...glad you're glad." He almost smacked his palm against his forehead for that winning response.

She gave him a little smile then directed her attention to the remnants of their lunch. Ginger crumbled up her sandwich wrapper and took one last sip from her drink. "Enough about me," she said with a serious tone. "We should get to the interview so I don't take up any more of your time." Her smile disappeared. Ginger had her notepad poised on her lap, ready to get back to business.

"You're not, but okay."

He loved that she'd opened up to him, even a little bit. It was like throwing back the curtains from inside a dark room. Ginger's light shone bright, and he could bask in it for as long as she kept talking.

The interview hadn't even started, but already she'd cut short their conversation when she started sharing her innermost thoughts. It was like she'd suddenly downloaded a security update and sharing anything personal was malware to be eliminated.

Cracking Ginger's firewall would take some creative troubleshooting, that's for sure. If only relationships were similar to decoding software, he'd be the guy to tackle it.

10

"When I need brain juice, Coffee Loft is the only way to go. It's like my home away from home, and that red velvet couch is the most perfect coffee-drinking spot on the planet." ~ Hairy Fairy

Talking with Cal anywhere except Coffee Loft had a profound effect on her freak-out meter.

It happened in the park the other day, and now here when she'd made the casual comment about the dog bowl. Lesson of the Day: keep all further communication with Cal at the shop unless she liked being caught off guard.

She tapped her pen on the notepad, willing the fluttering in her chest to go away. It didn't help that his eyes did some kind of hypnotic thing when he looked at her. Like she couldn't look away.

"Okay, so what three words would you use to describe

yourself?" She chanced a look, hoping to not find him staring again.

His brows knitted together, but he wore a poorly suppressed smile. "You're going to put that in the profile?"

"No, but it gives me a better sense of who you are. It will help warm me up when I start writing."

"Warm you up, I like th—"

"Three words, Cal." *If he'd just answer the question without the commentary.*

He squared his shoulders and looked into the fountain. After a minute, he ticked the first one off with a finger.

"Diligent."

"Good." She scribbled that down. "Two?"

"Funny, but not in a class-clown sort of way."

"That was more than one word."

"Some things beg for more of an explanation."

Smiling, she huffed and looked up at the sky. He really was funny in an understated sort of way. "Fine. What's the last one?"

"Introverted."

She looked at him through narrowed eyes. "I don't think so."

He let out a short bark of a laugh. "So, now you're editorializing?"

"Every time I see you on the patio, you're with a group of people." She laid her pen down and folded her hands over her notebook.

"That doesn't mean I love socializing 'round the clock."

"You could have fooled me."

"I work alone pretty much every day. The times when

you see me are during my lunch break, and most of the time I have a dog with me. The more chances I have to show them off in public, the more hope there is of them getting adopted."

"But it looks like you're enjoying yourself."

"I do love talking about the dogs, and meeting like-minded people," he said. Cal crossed his ankles and leaned back on his hands, looking straight ahead. "But the interactions wear me down after a while. My batteries get recharged when I'm alone."

He stared at her for an uncomfortably long time, like he was waiting for the information to soak in.

"Does that revelation alter your opinion of me?" he asked finally.

"Nope. Why would it?" *Gosh, his eyes are blue.*

"It appears you're thinking heavy thoughts," he said.

Yeah, like how your eyes are as bright as the blueberry bubble tea at the shop. Amazing.

"You're good at reading people, are you?"

Cal snorted. "No, not at all. I'm just good at feeling paranoid."

She chuckled as she wrote some nonsense on the page, phrases and random words she was certain wouldn't make a lick of sense when she reread it later. When she finished, she repositioned herself on the ledge.

"Next question. What do you like to do in your free time?"

He laughed off this question, too.

"Are you helping me write a dating profile or an impact statement for your application?"

She sighed. "Very funny."

"I volunteer at the shelter."

"I know that already. What else?"

"I read a lot. I'm a card-carrying library patron. I was a board member in the past, you know. And I fish."

She wrote that down, tucking a stray strand of hair behind her ear, until his running list of interests started coming too fast for her to keep up. She hooked her pen in the notebook's spiral spine and listened.

"Play Solitaire on my phone when I need to clear my head."

"Eat pizza."

"Collect L.A. Dodger baseball cards."

"Swim at the rec."

"Pick weeds out of my herb garden. There are more weeds than herbs, but I keep trying to find a bal—"

The sun glinted across the top of his head, revealing golden tones in his dark brown hair. He kept it shorter on the sides than he did on top. A neatly trimmed beard outlined his strong jaw—a good look for him. He bore a strong resemblance to some actor, but his name was on the tip of her tongue. She bet—

"Ginger?"

She jumped, launching her pen into the air. It landed at her feet.

"Sorry?" She picked it up, hoping that he attributed her reddened complexion to the exertion of bending over rather than being caught daydreaming. A forty-ish Brad Pitt. That's who he looked like. *Focus on the interview, Ginger.*

"I asked if you garden." He wore that smug smile again like he knew the effect he had on her.

"I don't. There's no room on my balcony."

"Container gardening is a thing, you know." He waved away his suggestion. "Anyway, I also have an old car that I tinker with when I have a spare minute. Which is never."

"Oh, yeah? My grandfather had a red Buick convertible that he kept in his barn. We used to ride in it when we'd visit. I loved riding in that thing with the top down."

"Mine's a 1952 Plymouth Cranbrook. I just had the interior redone, so that's all finished. There's quite a bit left to fix up on the exterior."

"There's something about old cars," she said. "I don't know the first thing about restoring one, but the memories..." She shook her head, smiling.

"Whenever I get it up and running, you'll be my first passenger," he said. "How's that?"

"I'd love it." She surprised herself with that answer, but honestly, she really wanted to ride in his car.

"It's a date, then."

She struggled to stop herself from grinning, so she dropped her gaze to the notes she'd dashed on the page. Funny how an innocent four-letter word like "date" could thrill her and make her breath hitch all in the same beat.

"*Three* dates on the calendar now." Her enthusiasm sounded forced even to her own ears.

"Is that a problem?" he asked with a hushed tone.

"Why should it be?" He didn't appear to be as flustered by this prospect as she was. Surely, he joked.

"Oh, I don't know. Maybe because you started frantically clicking your pen when I brought it up." He gently took the pen from her and set it down on the notebook. "This isn't a date, by the way. It's business. That should set your mind at ease."

"Thanks for clearing that up." *Yes, her imagination worked in overdrive, as usual.* She took an exaggerated deep breath. "Let's get back to the interview."

Cal nodded, folding his hands across his lap. "I'm ready."

"How has Coffee Loft impacted your life?"

"Professionally or personally?"

It sounded like a trick question. "Aren't they intertwined?"

"Not necessarily, but I'll give you what I think you want. Besides keeping me properly caffeinated, I'm thankful that you've allowed me to bring my dogs there."

"Go on." Surely, her face was back to doing a fine impersonation of a tomato. Compliments always made her blush; she couldn't help it.

"I can't think of another place in the area that makes me feel like I'm not imposing," he said in earnest. "You're very gracious and patient, considering the times the dogs have caused a ruckus."

"Like the time the rogue squirrel jumped onto one of the umbrellas from the awning and your dog went after it?" Luckily, only one other table had been occupied besides Cal's. She laughed at the memory.

He put his hands up on both sides of his face. "I was mortified. Or how about the time when that little Yorkie got her head stuck in the railing and I had to dismantle the bars?"

"During the mid-morning rush, no less." Ginger felt tears prick the corners of her eyes from laughing. "I almost banned you for life that day."

The smile dropped from his face. "Seriously?"

"I'm joking."

He slumped. "*Phew.*"

They shared a few seconds of silence before Cal cleared his throat.

"Mishaps aside, being able to bring the dogs to your place has made a difference. People who've stopped to talk with me have come into the shelter days later. I've never kept track of the dogs that have been adopted because of their appearance at Coffee Loft, but I have a feeling it's quite a few."

Now her vision clouded for a different reason. It warmed her heart to hear those words. And here she thought she was only serving coffee at the shop all along.

"Why did you start volunteering in the first place?"

"A friend got me started. She was the director at the shelter before the current one was hired. There was a shortage of volunteers, so I signed up to impress her," he said with a chuckle.

"You opportunist." She almost asked if they'd dated, but how was that relevant to the profile? A flutter in her chest at the thought of someone else competing for Cal's attention only confirmed it. *Not relevant at all.*

"Seriously though, I've always loved dogs," he continued. "It keeps me from working all day and into the night. I can be a little self-centered when it comes to work."

"Same." She stopped writing and raised her hand.

When she checked the time on her phone a short time later, she let out a yelp.

"We've been talking way too long."

"Who says?"

"You need to get back to work. I mean, I need to...*let* you get back to work."

He chuckled as he collected his lunch remnants. "You're the boss. Thanks for this, by the way."

"It's my pleasure." She stood, smoothed her skirt, and tucked the notebook into her bag.

"I can't tell you how much I appreciate this." She paused, already feeling like she'd taken too much of his time. "And the testimonial. If you could get it back to me soonish."

"I sure will." He looked down at her with a little smile. "I hope you win."

"We'll see." A deep sense of satisfaction for her work had nudged its way into her heart, thanks to Cal. She'd never fully realized that opening her patio to Cal's endless parade of pooches could have an impact on dogs and people alike.

"There's a monetary prize, isn't there? It's not just bragging rights?" he asked as he stood too.

"The top award is a ten-thousand-dollar grant. For business expansion, education, equipment. Four more people will also be chosen for smaller awards."

He nodded. "You've got this."

When they parted ways, she held her breath until he disappeared around the corner.

It'd been a surprising meeting, for sure. She'd expected to talk with Boisterous Cal. Flirty Cal. Instead, he'd answered her questions thoughtfully. He was funny, and charming, and so down-to-earth it seemed liked she'd known him forever. He'd left her wondering if she was wrong to peg him as a player. This revelation bothered her.

If she'd misread Cal for so long, how did that reflect on her?

11

If it weren't for the free parking in front, I never would have discovered this cute little coffee place. It's my favorite spot now to stop on Saturday mornings before the farmer's market. ~ Gretchen

Cal woke up a few days later feeling like he'd been run over by a truck.

If someone buffed his throat with sandpaper, it couldn't feel any worse, which wasn't ideal for a day when he'd scheduled meetings with two clients. Worse yet, he'd hoped to meet one of the clients at Coffee Loft. He'd been so swamped with work this week that he hadn't had a chance to visit.

Ginger's interview had only heightened his preoccupation with seeing her more. His daydreams were marked by scrolling images of her smile dimpling her cheeks; breezes sweeping her hair from her face; and how she'd press a hand against her chest sometimes when she laughed, like the happiness might bubble out of her body if she laughed too hard or too long. He was dying to see her again, but it wouldn't happen today. Not with whatever plagued him.

He sat up on the edge of his bed, grimacing. A ray of sunshine streaking in through a crack in the blinds made him wince. His head throbbed. The only comfort at the moment was the warm body nestled against his back. Ridley was the perfect snuggler. Once he started snoring, Cal knew he wouldn't move for the rest of the night. But now, he jumped down from the bed, stretched his hind legs one at a time, then sat and looked at Cal like, *what's taking you so long?*

"Sorry, Rid. Not feeling my chipper self today."

Ridley whined, walked a circle, and disappeared into the hallway. In the other room, bells jingled.

He smiled. Ridley had learned quickly how to let him know it was time to be let outside. The makeshift string of bells rang again as Cal dragged himself off the bed to open the door. Ridley loped across the brick patio. The shaded, fenced-in yard had been a major selling point when he bought the house, knowing his dogs would love to run.

After rummaging through the pantry then deciding to forgo breakfast for the time being, he padded outside in his bare feet. Settling into one of the patio chairs while Ridley continued his morning investigation around the yard, he checked his messages.

One of his clients had asked to reschedule. *Good.*

There was also a message from the shelter director, Charleen. *Call me ASAP please*, it read. Urgency was never a good sign when it came from Charleen.

"What's up?" he asked when Charleen answered the phone a few seconds later.

"Thanks for getting back to me so quickly. Listen, I have a special case for you."

"I'm listening."

"I got a call last night from a friend who knows of someone in desperate need of rehoming a dog."

"Go on."

"The dog is a thirteen-year-old Maltipoo. Her owner passed away. No one in the family can take this dog, so my friend reached out to see if we could help."

He hated cases like this because they truly wrenched his heart. Charleen knew this, which is why she always called Cal first.

"What's her temperament like?"

"'Sweet' is all my friend said. But she absolutely cannot stay in a kennel environment."

"No, I figured that, not at that age. Does she get along well with other dogs?"

"That I'm not sure of," Charleen said.

"I guess we'll see, then, won't we?"

"So you'll take her?"

Cal laughed. "Don't pretend you thought I wouldn't."

Charleen let out a sigh of relief. "You're a good man, Cal."

———

His symptoms worsened as the day wore on. As soon as the body aches hit shortly after he finished the Zoom call with the client, Cal eased himself onto the couch and pulled a throw across his body.

When he jolted awake, the sunlight in the room had shifted. Was it still the afternoon?

Someone rapped on the door. No doubt it was what had awoken him.

The realization that it was probably Charleen with his new friend hit him as he unfolded himself from the couch. His head heavy with sickness, he shuffled Ridley into the kitchen and put up a gate to cordon him off. Then he hurried to the door.

"Cal, I'm sorry to pop in, but——"

Ginger's tentative smile drooped when she saw him. He hadn't peered into a mirror since he stumbled out of bed that morning. It was safe to say he deserved the shocked look. But he was even more surprised to see her.

His erratic pulse skipped a few extra beats. He really needed to sit down. "I'm surprised to... I didn't know you were..."

Ginger took a step back. "I know. I'm sorry for not calling first. You haven't come in, so I thought I'd stop by and bring you this."

He hadn't noticed the coffee in her hand until she thrust it forward.

"Thank you." He took it, realizing he hadn't had any coffee yet today. He hadn't eaten anything, either. "I've been busy. Now sick." He pointed to his hair as if a bad case of bedhead was his most obvious symptom.

"Oh, I'm sorry. I definitely should have called."

"It's all right. I've just been sleeping all day." He leaned against the doorframe because he suddenly felt out of breath. The first sip of coffee was tasteless, but it soothed his throat. "I'd invite you in, but..."

Ginger's expression turned sympathetic. "Don't worry about it. It's completely understandable that you're not up for visiting." She flashed a smile. "Besides, we have the gala to look forward to. Gotta get better in time for that."

He felt so crummy, he couldn't even muster up the excitement of seeing Ginger at his doorstep for the first time. It'd surely hit him later. *But how did she know where I live?*

Behind her, a blue car pulled into Cal's driveway. Ginger turned to look and stood rooted in place as Charleen got out, opened her hatch, and pulled out a portable dog carrier. She turned back to him with her brows raised.

"Company?" she asked.

"A new and hopefully very temporary foster."

Charleen slowed as she stepped onto the porch.

"Cal, you don't look like you're up for this," Charleen said with a look of concern.

His head swam, but it was nothing compared to what this poor dog was going through.

"I'll be fine. What's her name?" He squatted to see inside the carrier. Two shining, dark eyes and a mass of white hair were all that was visible.

"Meet Peaches. I have her other things in the car," Charleen said, hooking a thumb over her shoulder. "Sorry, but I need to run. There are two intakes coming in within the next hour."

Cal hoisted the carrier over to the rocking chair where he could sit on the far end of the porch. He opened the latch and, luckily, he had both hands in front of the door, or she would have bolted and disappeared through the porch railings.

"Whoa," Ginger cried. She'd been silently taking it all in until Peaches' near-escape. "She's a little white bullet."

Charleen hauled two stuffed garbage bags, filled with enough dog paraphernalia to stock one of the national pet store chains, onto the porch.

"Here we go," Charleen said, planting the bags at his feet. "I also have a big bag of her food. The family felt guilty—"

"—guilty enough to buy out all the PetsMore franchises in the Midwest?"

"It's more like all of them west of the Mississippi," Ginger added under her breath.

He and Charleen looked at her in unison, which made Cal realize his mistake.

"Ginger, this is Charleen, director of Hearts Fur Love. Charleen, my friend Ginger."

"I've been a longtime customer at Coffee Loft, but it's nice to formally meet you," Charleen said. "Are you interested in fostering a dog?"

He pretended not to see Ginger blanch.

"I have a cat," she said, invoking her ready-made excuse.

"That's not a problem. Peaches grew up with cats. Adores them," Charleen said. She looked at Cal. "The family kept the cats, but not poor Peaches."

"I'll make her as comfortable as possible and do a meet-and-greet with Ridley as soon as I'm up for it." He found a leash inside the bag and handed it to Charleen who clipped it onto the dog's collar while he held Peaches in his arms.

"Thanks so much," Charleen said, backing down the steps. "Please call with a report tonight if you have time, Ginger, nice to meet you."

He and Ginger watched Charleen's little car wheel out of the driveway and disappear at the end of the block. Ginger, who'd grown quiet when Charleen mentioned Peaches and her cat siblings, cleared her throat.

"I wouldn't know the first thing to do with a dog."

"Food, water, exercise, companionship. That's all they need."

"Don't forget vet appointments and grooming." She looked down at the garbage bags stuffed to the brim. "And apparently enough toys to warrant adding another room onto your house."

He stood, intending to carry Peaches into the house and get her used to the sights and smells of Chez Donner. Ridley, no doubt, would go bonkers. But when he stood, he wobbled on his feet and unintentionally landed back in his seat with a heavy thud.

"Cal! What's wrong?"

Ginger rushed to him, almost tripping over Peaches' cage. Instead, she caught her knee on the little side table.

"*Oh!*" She bent over double.

"Careful!" He extended his arm, but she was well past needing a steady hand. Clutching her knee, she cried out in pain...then landed in his lap.

OOOF!

Their eyes met briefly, then hers widened with horror. She popped up faster than a malware alert.

"I'm so sorry. Did I hurt you?" Her complexion matched

the fire engine squeaky toy peeking out the top of Peaches' bag.

"I'm fine." He laughed despite the drumbeat in his temples. She was as weightless as Peaches. Of course, she didn't hurt him, but he wished he felt well enough to relish the moment.

"I should let you get back to doing what you were doing," she said, rubbing her knee. She shook her head, still flustered. "I'm just in the way."

On the contrary, he wished she were more in the way, *his* way.

"Thanks for the coffee. It's good relief for the throat."

That seemed to set her at ease. She took a big breath. "You're welcome," she said with a nod. "I also came by to let you know I submitted the application, too."

"Great. When will you hear?"

"Two weeks." She bounced on the balls of her feet.

"Have you thought about how you'll use the money if you win."

She chewed on her lip, thinking. "I've been mulling over the idea of a mobile truck for a while. I don't want to necessarily commit to opening another brick and mortar location, so a truck feels right at this point."

"There are plenty of coffee deserts around town."

She nodded. "I've been doing my research."

Of course, she had. He loved her get-up-and-go attitude.

Tugging on the leash, Peaches whined. She splayed her legs in front of her with her rump in the air.

He tipped his chin toward Peaches. "Look at that. She wants to play with you."

"But...but I didn't do anything." Ginger looked skeptical. She even stepped toward the stairs.

"You must be a dog lover at heart. They can sense those things."

"Maybe Peaches' people-picker is off." Ginger extended a hand toward the dog who promptly slathered it with kisses. "I've never had a dog, so that should be a warning to her."

He struggled out of the chair. "I'd better get her inside."

"Are you sure you're okay? Can I pick up anything at the store?"

"I've got a whole medicine cabinet filled with stuff I never use. Best to just ride it out, whatever it is. But thank you." Her concern and attentiveness touched him. Ginger's forehead creased as Peaches wrapped the leash around his legs.

"Will Ridley mind her?" Ginger asked. She stared at Peaches, but he could tell her thoughts were far beyond the confines of his front porch.

"I have no idea." He short-leashed the little dog until he could untangle himself. "Ridley tolerated Lola. Before her, Ridley hadn't been vetted around other dogs. It's always a gamble."

"All relationships are, I suppose," Ginger said under her breath, but loudly enough that he caught it. Still distracted, Ginger's expression changed when Peaches approached again and sniffed her shoe. She bent down to ruffle the dog's head. "Call if you need anything."

"Thanks. I will."

Cal scooped Peaches into his arms; he'd get the rest of her

things later. He stood in the doorway, watching Ginger drive away.

She hadn't only come to deliver a coffee. But with the chaos surrounding Peaches' arrival and him not feeling well, he didn't want to press her.

All relationships are a gamble, she'd said.

With the gala just a few weeks away, there wasn't much time to see if their relationship would pay off.

12

"*Our book group has been meeting at Coffee Loft for two years now. Ginger and crew keep our drink orders coming AND put up with our rowdiness. CL, we love you!*" - the Madhatters

Ginger tapped a foot as she waited for the receptionist to call her and Daisy into one of the rooms the next day. With the application deadline and prepping Coffee Loft for the fall festival taking up most of her time this past week, she'd almost forgotten Daisy's appointment for her annual shots that morning. Beside her on the floor in her carrier, Daisy mournfully peeked at her through the wire door.

"Daisy?"

A young vet assistant ushered her back into one of the rooms and weighed Daisy. While she prepped the vaccine on the other side of the room, Ginger held onto the squirming cat.

Doctor Robinson walked into the room a short time later. She'd come highly recommended when Ginger moved to Port Chance. They shared a birthday, she'd discovered, and a fondness for Maine Coon cats.

"Ginger, hello. How's the coffee business?" Dr. Robinson draped a towel across the examination table. She signaled for Ginger to bring Daisy.

"Busy. I haven't seen you in a while." She soothed Daisy with scratches where it mattered most: between her ears. Daisy fought to keep her eyes open.

"My husband bought me one of those fancy espresso machines for my birthday, though I think it was just as much a gift for him as it was for me."

"Nice."

"I shouldn't complain. It's divine having a latte ready and waiting for me as soon as I step out of the shower every morning." Dr. Robinson's assistant held Daisy's back end while the doctor administered the shot. They were finished in a blink without a hiss from Daisy this time.

"You should stop in to see the fall merchandise before I switch it out for the holidays. We have the cutest coffee bar accessories on display this season. Adorable wooden organizers, ceramic trivets."

"I will. I've been craving a pumpkin chai for days now anyway."

Dr. Robinson ran her hands along Daisy's coat, lifting her chin, checking her ears and teeth. When she finished, Ginger lifted Daisy from the table and tucked her back into the carrier.

"I keep forgetting to tell you we have an acquaintance in common," Dr. Robinson said. "Cal Donner?"

"Yes, I know Cal. He's a long-time customer." That buzzy sensation gripped her again like it did whenever Cal popped into her thoughts lately. Which was *a lot*.

"I know. I ran into him a few weeks ago as he was leaving your patio. What a great guy."

"He is." The grin she'd pasted on her face felt overdone, even a little manic.

"And he's such a rockstar in the shelter world," Dr. Robinson gushed.

"He's definitely found his calling. Everyone gravitates toward him when he brings his dogs to the shop."

"I'm sure. Do you follow him online?"

She let Merris handle social media for the shop since she was much more in tune to that sort of thing. Merris enjoyed it, so it was a win-win that Ginger didn't have to bother.

"No, I don't."

Dr. Robinson put a hand against her chest. "Oh, my goodness. You have to see it. Here," she said, fishing her phone from her back pocket.

When Cal's profile appeared, she almost didn't recognize him. The photos looked professional-grade, for one. They were colorful and alive, full of movement and joy.

Selfies with dogs of all sizes and colors she didn't recognize.

Cal lying on a blanket outside with Ridley.

Cal and Lola.

Cal next to a mop bucket, posing like he was on the red carpet instead of in a kennel.

On Coffee Loft's patio.

Next to the Hearts Fur Love sign.

Gobs of people surrounding him, like he was the sun to their solar system.

Hundreds of photos.

"He has forty-two *thousand* followers?" Her shop had a tiny fraction of that amount. She'd had a celebrity in her midst this whole time.

"Isn't that incredible?" Dr. Robinson's eyes popped. "The best part are the stories he tells. If you get a chance, take a look at some of his posts."

"I had no idea." Of course, she didn't. She'd been too focused on pre-conceived opinions before she really got to know him.

Dr. Robinson slipped her phone back into her pocket. "He advocates so much for dogs and adopting. It's hard not to love the guy."

"I know."

Who was she kidding? Exactly what did she know?

Apparently, nothing.

Before she interviewed him, she didn't know one morsel of truth about Cal Donner, that's what. *Wait—let's take that back.* He liked café au laits, so she knew *something*. But even now, she'd discovered yet another facet—a huge one, at that— that had escaped her. Full of surprises, he was. And the more she learned about him, the more she couldn't get him off her mind.

Merris stood behind the counter with the new hire, Alice, as Ginger walked into the shop after dropping Daisy off at home.

"How's training going?" She set the tube holding the signs for the Fall Days Festival on the counter and greeted her two employees. "Are you ready to take over operations yet?" she asked Alice.

Alice laughed nervously. "Maybe by next week?"

"She's almost memorized the entire drink menu," Merris said. "It took me weeks."

"I've been studying," Alice said with a sheepish grin. Her tight braids accentuated her dark eyes and the upward slashes of her brows.

"So maybe you *will* be ready," she assured her.

As a new college graduate, Alice hadn't yet found a job related to her business degree, she'd told Ginger during her interview last week. She'd waitressed, worked at a home improvement store, and she was bored, frustrated, and going broke fast, she'd said.

Had Merris not recommended her, Ginger probably wouldn't have hired Alice. She'd displayed a lack of confidence in herself during their conversations that seemed self-sabotaging. She'd also told Ginger that she dreamed of having her own coffee truck one day, hopping around the country to art fairs and farmer's markets. Would she want to spend all this time training Alice only to lose her in a few months if another opportunity presented itself? Her employees were like family. She paid them very well and offered perks that other food establishments would find hard to top. She did this so she could retain the people she'd invested in. Turnover at Coffee Loft was next to nothing. Ginger liked to keep it that way. Initial reservations aside, she'd hired Alice the next day.

"I'll need all the help I can get today and tomorrow with Fall Days Festival this weekend." She popped the cap off the tube to pull out the posters that she'd picked up from the printer, unrolling one. She held it up. "What do you think?"

"Eye-catching!" Alice said.

Merris opened her mouth to say something, but snapped it shut. She peered closer at the poster. "Did you design it?"

"Not technically, but I offered my input when the Chamber people asked. Why?"

"Like, did you say, 'Put a guy and a woman at a café table together who look like Cal Donner and me'?"

"What?!" Ginger turned the poster around to look, her heart pounding.

Yes, there was a couple on the poster, though their profiles were all wrong. She'd never wear heels to work. And purple earrings? Big nope. The man's swooping coif stamped him as a Hollywood type despite her discovery that Cal didn't have an ounce of pretentiousness in his body.

"They look nothing like me and Cal."

Merris snickered. "Ginger has a secret admirer who visits the shop regularly."

She sighed. "It's not so secret since you harass me about him constantly."

"Do not."

She nodded slowly. "All. The. Time."

Wisely, Alice stayed silent.

"Sometimes he leaves her notes on the patio table. It's so

cute." Merris dug into her apron pocket. "I think I have one from the other day still in my pocket. Yep, here it is."

Ginger snatched the note and buried it in her own pocket without reading it. "For all I know it's you who's been writing them."

"Me?!" Merris feigned shock. "For one, that's not my handwriting."

She replaced the cap on the poster tube and handed it to Merris, hoping a task would shut her up.

"I need these taped onto the front door, the placard which is in the office, and the windows facing the patio, please."

"You've got it, boss." Merris's cheeks plumped up with her barely contained smile.

She watched Merris cross the lobby to the front doors, with Alice following closely behind. Grinning, she shook her head. Brushing off Merris's teasing had become so inconsequential that she paid it no mind. Merris and jokes were like bread and butter, so common that the day wouldn't be the same with one and not the other.

But as a certain someone took up more and more of her head space lately, she felt herself growing self-conscious. A mere mention of Cal made her pulse buzz like a bee hive. And when she did see him, her body acted of its own accord, with all sorts of strange beats and twitches, contrary to her brain saying, *stop!*

Since he dropped off his testimonial the day before he got sick, she'd read it at least a dozen times so far. It was praise for Coffee Loft, but she couldn't help wondering if he'd specifically thought of her as he wrote it. She could almost hear him speak as she read phrases like "it's not just a destination, but an experience, thanks to Ginger Giatti's vision" and "the personable owner and her gift for hospitality make Coffee Loft the best coffee spot in the county." It infused her with a warmth that stayed with her throughout the day.

Now the question was this: what was she going to do about it?

She was unpacking that morning's delivery of to-go containers and cups, mulling over her options, when Merris poked her head in the back room, wide-eyed.

"Ridley's on the patio. Without Cal."

13

So many accolades for Coffee Loft! Customer service is top notch, the drinks are amazing, and the atmosphere is what every coffee shop should strive for. ~ 123Gimme Coffee

Sure enough, Cal's horse-dog had parked himself at their usual table, despite a couple sitting there who now found themselves with a furry audience while they sipped their cappuccinos.

Her heart hammered in her chest at the unexpected sight. What had happened to Cal that allowed Ridley to appear all by himself?

She hurried outside to find Ridley's head in the man's lap. By all outward appearances, it looked like the dog was doing a solid job as Coffee Loft's canine ambassador, if there was such a thing. However, Ginger knew Ridley. *You're in my guy's seat* was more likely Ridley's unspoken message.

"I'm so sorry," she said as she ruffled Ridley's back to coax him away.

To their credit, the man and woman took it in stride. "We're dog lovers, so it's no problem," the man said.

When Ridley showed no signs of budging, she took off her belt, looped it inside Ridley's collar, and fastened it for a makeshift leash. With Ridley in tow, she met Merris at the door.

"Can you get them a ten-dollar gift card? I'm going to run Ridley home."

"I hope Cal's okay," said Merris.

"I'm sure Ridley just escaped." She wished she was as confident of that as her words implied. "I'll be back as soon as I can."

It'd be faster to walk him home than maneuver the big oaf up her stairs and into her apartment so she could grab her car keys. As she started down the sidewalk toward Cal's house, so many scenarios played havoc with her mind. Was he lying face down somewhere with Ridley's leash in hand? Was he feeling worse, maybe on his deathbed, and forgot Ridley in the backyard, and somehow the dog escaped? Her imagination was on a roll.

When she arrived at Cal's house, the drawn blinds and closed garage door didn't hint at anything out of the ordinary. She knocked and listened for his footsteps.

Nothing.

She knocked again. At her side, Ridley whined and pawed at the door.

"It's okay, buddy." She pressed his immense head against her hip to reassure him like she'd seen Cal do on occasion, and knocked one more time. "I'm sure your dad is fine."

At least I hope he is.

Ridley whined again when they heard the bark inside. He scratched again at the door, this time more frantically.

"Cal?" she called as she rattled the doorknob, expecting it to be locked.

But it swung inward.

Ridley tugged her inside. She lost her grip on the belt as he bolted down the hallway, running deeper into the house.

She called for Cal again as she eyed Peaches locked in her crate in the dining room, looking at her with wide moon eyes underneath her scruffy mop of hair.

She returned to his foyer to stand on his welcome mat and wondered what to do. If only she'd brought her phone, but she'd left it on her desk in the office. She kept reminding herself to breathe. *Where could he be?*

A car engine revved in the driveway as she crossed the dining room to the patio door to check the backyard. She stopped in her tracks, then rushed to the window to peer through the front curtains. Cal hurried up the sidewalk.

He threw open the half-closed door with confusion crinkling his brow, and stopped on the welcome mat just as she rushed to him, throwing her arms around him.

"Cal! I was worried sick!"

She pulled away almost as quickly as she'd hugged him. Shock and relief infused her senses, pounding through her chest, pushing the blood through her veins as though her body just now came alive again.

"You were? Wh-where'd you find him?" He steadied her

with his hands on her arms. He still looked sick. His eyes were puffy and his was nose was red, but he'd shaved and traded his sweatpants for jeans.

"He came to Coffee Loft. We found him on the patio."

Cal closed the door behind him as he shot Ridley a dirty look.

"*You* about gave me a heart attack," he said, pointing a finger at the dog. He unhooked Ginger's belt from Ridley's collar and handed it back to her with a grin. "Ingenious thinking."

"It was one of my finer moments." She strung it back through her belt loops then tucked her hands in her pockets. "What happened?"

"The back gate somehow was left open. A few neighbors have mentioned things being taken, people caught on camera trespassing in backyards." He sighed. "I hate to think someone would leave it unlocked on purpose."

"You'll have to put a padlock on it to be safe."

"I've already bought one."

"Thank goodness he had the sense to come to the shop." She pulled her hand out of her pocket and rested it against her neck, feeling her pulse returning to normal.

Cal bent down to retrieve something from the carpet.

"This fell out of your pocket," he said, but pulled it back and unfolded the little slip of paper. He looked at it for a moment, grinning, before offering it to her again. "I think this is yours."

It was the note that Merris claimed was the latest one left by Cal. She'd forgotten about it after finding Ridley on the patio. Now she read it, feeling the smile spread across her face.

Hope you have a doggone great day! Ridley, Peaches, and Cal.

He'd turned the dot on the exclamation point into a heart with a smiley face.

"Too obnoxious, my notes?" he asked with laughter in his tone.

"On the contrary, they make my day."

"Yeah?"

She nodded.

Sometimes the truth took longer to recognize, especially when egos were on the line. But this time, Cal's sweet little missive hit her heart in just the right spot, revealing a thin ray of light that had broken through the dark void.

14

Love you guys! Thanks for starting my mornings out right! ~ Cassie

Three hours, maybe four.

That wasn't enough sleep for Cal to survive the day. His dash around town yesterday looking for Ridley hadn't helped. The stuffiness in his head came back full-force overnight. But no one could keep him away from Coffee Loft and Ginger today, not with the hopeful sign from her in his living room. That hug was like a double shot of espresso. Man, could he use another one now.

Cal lumbered down the sidewalk, led by a hyper, four-legged white mop. Peaches garnered so many *awww*s during the four-block stroll to Coffee Loft, he might as well be pushing a chubby-cheeked baby in a stroller rather than trailing after a mutt on a leash.

Peaches steered him around the iron fence when they got to Coffee Loft's patio.

How did she know that?

None of the other tables were occupied, thank goodness. He wasn't up for socializing today.

He collapsed in a chair, blowing his nose while he contemplated Peaches' uncanny ability of knowing his destination, when Ginger appeared on the patio.

"You must be feeling—" Ginger paused when he looked up, then thrust her bottom lip out. "I take that back. You look like you pulled an all-nighter."

At his feet, Peaches perked her ears up at the sound of Ginger's voice.

"An all-nighter with two dogs that don't get along."

"Oh, Cal. I'm so sorry."

"And this flu or cold, whatever it is, is beating me up." He almost didn't have the energy to even shrug. "I'm getting better, but not fast enough."

"I take it Ridley's in the doghouse for the stunt he pulled?"

He groaned. "I feel like I can almost swap stories with my sister about unruly teenagers with what that dog has put me through."

Ginger giggled and put her finger up. "I'll be right back."

Peaches tugged on the leash, trying to follow Ginger back into the shop.

He reeled her in. "You little traitor. She doesn't even like dogs."

One of the two women walking by on the sidewalk eyed him suspiciously until she noticed Peaches.

"Awww," she cooed.

Her friend spotted Peaches, too. "Hi, baby," she said as they walked by.

He couldn't even muster a smile. Little did they know Peaches was a tyrant in disguise.

"Here you go."

Ginger was back, and she set a mug of steaming pink something in front of him. A leaf floated on the top.

"What is it?"

"Elderberry tea. I just got it in. It's part of my new health and wellness tea display."

"Thanks, but I'm not really a fan—"

"Drink it," she said in a no-nonsense tone he hadn't heard before. She softened when he looked at her, startled. "It'll knock your symptoms down."

He leaned over the mug. It didn't smell so bad.

She pulled out a chair and sat with Cal. "If you prefer, I can put it over ice."

He leaned back in his chair as he took the mug, letting the steam waft over his face. "Not necessary."

He sipped. The stuff soothed his throat, he'd give it that.

Ginger watched him, waiting for a reaction.

"Not as bad as you thought?"

"Tolerable." He took another sip, then set the mug down. "I prefer my café au laits."

"Of course, you do. But stay away from milk until this clears." She circled her finger around her nose and mouth. "Dairy won't help your congestion."

He rubbed his beard stubble, not even caring that Ginger was seeing the worst version of himself at the moment.

"Tell me about the dog situation," Ginger said.

"Ridley wants to eat Peaches." When Ginger gasped, he figured he should clarify. "Like, in a friendly sort of way."

Her blank stare meant she didn't quite get how eating a household member could be considered anything other than hostile.

"And you're keeping them separated, right?"

"Oh, gosh, yes. It'd be World War Three if I didn't. Peaches wouldn't stand for it."

As if Peaches sensed she was the topic of conversation, she put her front paws on Ginger's knees. He tried to move her away, but Ginger lifted her onto her lap instead. His mouth almost fell open. This was the most interest Ginger had shown any of his dogs. *Ever.*

"Are you being a bad little girl?" Ginger whispered. Peaches responded by licking Ginger's nose with her pink, darting tongue. Ginger giggled, then set her back down on the bricks.

Incredulous, he gaped at her. "What just happened here?"

"What?" Ginger said, brushing off her pants.

"You actually touched her. You let her lick you without recoiling."

Ginger considered this, glancing at Peaches with a look that could only be described as lovey-dovey.

"I feel bad for her."

He took another sip of Ginger's tea concoction. Funny, it was beginning to grow on him. He plucked out the leaf garnish and set it on the saucer.

"She's in good hands. Peaches just needs to get used to

the idea that Ridley is a sweetheart, and let me get a decent night's sleep." He sighed. "They literally barked at each other all night long."

"Oh, Cal," she said. "No wonder you look...like you haven't slept."

"Nice save." He chuckled. *Looked like something at the bottom of a dumpster*, she might have said. Or better yet, *looked like something you'd pick up with a doggie bag*.

Ginger grimaced like he'd read her mind, but her gaze softened.

"We apparently share the same vet, you know," she said out of nowhere.

"Oh, yeah? Dr. Robinson. She's a wonderful human."

"She's sure full of compliments for you, too. Said you've found your niche."

He felt a sneeze coming on. Scrambling for the tissue he'd stuffed in his pocket, he knew he wouldn't get it in time. Too late. Instead, he sneezed into the crook of his arm.

Ginger left the table in a hurry. He didn't fault her. What person in her right mind wanted to hang around a walking germ factory like himself?

A minute later, she was back with a tissue box. She set it in front of him and reclaimed her spot across the table. Normally, she was in a hurry to get back to work. But today Ginger seemed like she was pointedly trying to avoid it.

Huh.

"Thank you." He took a tissue. "Anyway, I'd like to think I've found my calling."

"You're lucky. Not many people do."

He studied her. She'd frowned when she said that. "Is there something wrong?"

"I don't know. I guess it got me thinking about what my niche is, too. What am I passionate about?"

"Making coffee, of course. Making people happy, giving them a place to socialize, or just find a little peace in the midst of a chaotic day."

"I suppose." She shook her head, dismissing it. "But I don't think it's enough anymore."

"Why not? You have no idea what this means to people." He opened his arms, gesturing to the expanse of the patio and the building. It was enough for him. But, then again, not every Coffee Loft customer coming for a caffeine fix also daydreamed about the owner. "What's changed?"

"Watching you in your element, I guess." She smiled while her tone dripped with friendly sarcasm.

"You wouldn't be the first person whose life changed course because of me." He could dish it right back.

She grinned—one of those real ones which he didn't see too often—but when he did, it melted his core like a marshmallow over a campfire.

"I'd better get back," she said, standing. Peaches took the opportunity to stand with her, waggling her behind.

Not so soon, please. "What do you have going on today?"

"Mostly training," Ginger said as she studied Peaches, "but the Fall Days Festival is Saturday, so I have to figure out what I'm doing for that."

"Saturday is *soon.*"

"I know. I'm way behind."

"Do you need help?"

"You don't look like you're up for anything more than sleeping for the next forty-eight hours."

"At this point, I'd settle for a two-hour nap." He reeled Peaches in on her leash.

"I can take Peaches for a few hours."

Wait, what?

The craziness of her suggestion actually made him lean back against his seat. Was she mad?

"You hate dogs."

She snorted. "I don't *hate* dogs. I've just never had one." She lifted her chin, a little indignant.

"A self-rec like that doesn't make me want to turn her over to you anytime soon." He'd meant it as a joke, but hurt registered on her face.

"You're right. I wouldn't entrust her to me, either."

Now he felt like he'd taken it too far. "I'm sorry. I'm joking. But Charleen wouldn't allow it anyway without a volunteer form."

"That's okay," she said quietly as she backed away.

"Ginger?"

She stopped. "Yes?"

"I appreciate the offer." It was so out of character.

She studied Peaches for a moment as another frown pulled at the corners of her mouth.

"I know. I guess I feel sorry for her. Like, she thought she was set for life, feeling safe and loved. And then it was gone." Her chest rose and fell with a deep sigh.

He had a feeling this wasn't just about Peaches.

"What do I owe you for the tea?"

Ginger waved away the question. "On the house."

"Every drink you give me lately is on the house."

She answered him with a smile innocent enough in the general sense, but coming from her, directed toward *him*, well, it lit a little fire in him, runny nose and scratchy throat aside. Whatever she did lately had that effect.

Wait. Correction.

Ginger's impact surprised him the first time he set eyes on her. The difference between then and now was it just kept skyrocketing.

15

Prepare to be enlightened at your visit to Coffee Loft. It's a real gem. ~ L. Ridman

She left Cal on the patio, the sting of his comment still piercing her heart as she made her way through the shop. He'd claimed it was a joke—she was a self-professed cat person, wasn't she?—but it hurt nonetheless.

Ginger retreated to her office to take inventory of the supplies she'd set aside for the fall festival, hoping to take her mind off Cal. She pulled down two plastic tubs and removed the lid from the first one. The twelve origami floral center-pieces she'd found at the downtown art fair back in June, one for each table, surprised her. She'd completely forgotten them. In the other tub, she'd stashed tea and coffee samples for giveaways, along with the cute insulated mugs with leaf motifs. There was more decor and merchandise that she'd forgotten about, probably more than she needed. She still had to make signs for the sale table and have Merris redo the seasonal drink board with the new drinks to debut for the weekend. Maybe she was more organized than she'd originally thought.

Glancing at her to-do list on the desk, Cal's glossy black business card caught her attention instead. It peeked out from underneath the paper tablet where she'd left it the night she called him about the interview. She pulled it out.

Cal not jumping on her offer to dog sit Peaches shouldn't bother her as much as it did. It was impulsive on her part, and thank goodness he had the sense to know that. Still, she'd wanted to help.

Is that all you want, Ginger?

She stared at his card while the overhead light caught its sheen.

No, helping Cal wasn't all she wanted.

Be honest now.

She loved his selfless commitment to the shelter. It wasn't something that she'd thought about deeply until she interviewed him. Was her sudden appeal to watch Peaches an attempt to meet Cal on common ground?

The storm changed everything. He'd shown her a part of himself she'd never seen before. And it'd made her more curious than ever. But she was such an expert at keeping him at arm's length, thanks to her ex-husband, that she hadn't taken the next step.

She picked up her phone and tapped the icon of her new social media app, the one she'd asked Alice to help her download after the vet appointment. She'd only read a handful of Cal's posts, but she couldn't get enough of his photos.

Scrolling through his images, she stopped on one of her favorite photos.

It was a close-up of him hugging Ridley. He wore sunglasses and a wide smile. Ridley's nose was so close it took up almost half the photo. It was the kind of image that made you smile long after you stopped looking at it.

She scanned a dozen more photos until a photo of Ridley wearing a top hat made her stop scrolling again. Next to him, practically tucked underneath his front leg, was a little tan-and-white dog, a Jack Russell terrier, the caption explained, wearing a double strand of pearls.

If I were a dog, I'd want to be just like my pal, Ridley, Cal had written. *No matter who I bring into the house, he's such a welcoming host. Wilhelmina, the proper little lady next to him in the photo, is a perfect example. While they might seem like the best of friends here, she wanted no part of him on day one.*

Funny. That sounded familiar. She continued reading.

These two are now inseparable. Like a quirky old couple you'd see sitting on their front porch as you passed by in your car. I might be so lucky someday, finding my soulmate. Without the wet nose and twitchy ears, of course—

"Ginger!" Merris whisper-hissed right over her left shoulder.

She whirled around, tucking her phone into the folds of her jacket. Her heart landed in her throat, rendering her speechless for a few seconds.

"What is it?" She tried to ignore the smugness on

Merris's face. Merris had seen what had Ginger so consumed, no doubt.

"Cal needs to see you."

"Again?"

She nodded. "He's still on the patio."

"Well, what does he want?"

Merris shrugged. "Didn't ask, and he didn't tell."

He leaned against a light post when Ginger made it back outside, looking like he was one cough away from an urgent care visit.

"Listen, please don't agree to this if it's not truly what you want," he started to say until a coughing fit interrupted him. Ginger bent over to pet Peaches while he fought to regain control of his voice.

"I talked to Charleen about...your offer—"

"What offer?"

She knew what he alluded to, but playing dumb gave her a few extra seconds to process it. An arrow of panic rushed through her. She'd already dismissed the silly notion of watching his dog for a few hours when he nixed the idea. Now he was about to take her up on it.

What have I gotten myself into?

"You volunteered to watch Peaches for a bit? Unless you're having second thoughts."

Her mind was a blank canvas. No words, no thoughts, nothing.

"And, listen. I really am sorry about the self-rec comment. It was a poor attempt at a little humor."

But he looked so desperate, and she truly wanted to help.

"Don't worry about it. I...I was just preoccupied with organizing the office. I thought you'd left."

"Charleen said I could fill out the volunteer form and have you sign it. She knows I'll vouch for you." He smiled weakly, though it still had the same effect on her as his full-watt grin. This time it helped dispel the doubts that this bona fide cat person couldn't dog sit for a few hours.

"Happy to help," she said, bracing herself for the adventure. Daisy was going to flat out revolt. "I can swing by to get her after work."

Cal pressed a hand against his heart. "Thank you so much."

———

Ginger eyed Peaches through the bedroom door as she sat at the kitchen counter catching up on paperwork later that night. The old girl walked three circles in the center of her bed then lay down in a tight ball, keeping her sad, watchful eyes on Ginger the whole time. To her credit, Peaches was still pretty spry for her age. She'd leapt onto the bed with little effort as soon as she'd finished a thorough investigation of the rooms. And to Ginger's surprise, Daisy hadn't caused a ruckus yet, though her expression told Ginger she wasn't thrilled with the situation.

When she'd shown up at Cal's home earlier, he'd handed her a pink quilted bag filled with snacks and toys for Peaches.

"She's been hiding under the dining room table since I brought her back home. I'm not sure this will work," he'd said.

He'd looked so tired. The bags under his eyes had only deepened since that afternoon.

"Peaches," she'd called. Little feet skittered on the hardwood floor a few seconds later, and a white blur tore around the corner, flying toward Ginger.

"I don't think it'll be a problem," she'd said. The relief on Cal's face when he saw Peaches reaction to her made the dog hair and bad breath she'd have to endure more than worthwhile.

Now Ginger tried to focus on the spreadsheet in front of her, but Peaches kept drawing her attention.

"I'm sorry, Peaches."

The dog's ears pricked.

She left the kitchen counter to settle next to the dog on the bed. When she laid a hand on the dog's back, the dog shook intermittently.

"You poor thing." She stroked her fur and hummed the first song that came to mind, a Billy Joel tune that had been playing in Coffee Loft as she left for the day. "You're all out of sorts, aren't you?"

She felt the bed shift behind her back. Soon enough, Daisy hopped over her legs, landing in front of her and Peaches. She settled on her haunches, the tip of her tail switching back and forth.

"What?"

Daisy meowed and blinked.

"You could be a little more welcoming, you know."

Blink.

Ginger knew this dog-sitting thing would be all-consuming, but now that she was in the thick of it, ensuring

Peaches' comfort wasn't so much a burden as it was a priority.

Her phone buzzed on the nightstand. She sat up, crossing her legs when Cal's name showed on the screen.

"How's she doing?" he asked as soon as she answered the call.

"She's a little nervous. I think Daisy might surprise me, though. I'm expecting her to roll out the welcome mat any minute now." She eyed Daisy who'd stretched into a sphinx position, looking ready to pounce.

"It's only been three hours," Cal said. "The first three days are the most traumatic, and it can take up to three weeks for a shelter dog to start feeling at home."

"That's a long time." She resumed stroking Peaches. "On the bright side, you sound better."

"A power nap does wonders," he rasped in a throaty whisper that made his already deep voice even more appealing.

"I'm glad it worked."

"Is now a good time to pick her up?" he asked.

She paused with her hand on Peaches' back. Daisy extended her body to its full length, stretching toward the dog. Peaches, in turn, slowly met Daisy's nose with her own. It was a split-second acknowledgement, but it warmed her heart. The endearing sight almost prompted her to lie alongside them and join in with a group hug.

"I can't believe it."

"What?" Cal asked.

"I think I just witnessed Daisy's version of a peace offering."

"I'm jealous. Is she for hire?"

She scratched Daisy between her ears. "Maybe Peaches just needed to start with someone her own size. Ridley can be a scary moose."

"I'll give you moose, but he's far from scary," he said with a chuckle.

"Can I keep her overnight?" she blurted.

There was a lengthy pause.

"Hello?" Had the call disconnected?

"I'm here. My ears might be plugged," he said. "Did you seriously just ask for a sleepover with Peaches?"

"Is that a bad idea?" Maybe she was asking for trouble, or at least a sleepless night, but the sweet exchange she'd just witnessed raised her hopes for helping Peaches feel better, and in the larger picture, Cal.

"Only you can answer that," he answered. Was it her imagination or had Cal's tone changed? He sounded... awestruck.

"Let's try. Do you have to run it by Charleen again?"

"No," Cal said. "The form you signed means you're an official foster."

She sat up straight. "An official foster. This is a big deal." She should take ownership of this. Maybe Coffee Loft could sponsor something for the shelter.

"It is. Even if your only reason is to help me out."

"I...I think it's a bit more than that." Her bubble deflated a little.

"Well, I do appreciate it. And I can be there in no time if you need rescuing."

Rescuing.

She liked the sound of that.

After she hung up, she watched Peaches and Daisy make more tentative strides toward one another. Peaches laid her paw over Daisy's paw. Daisy circled Peaches and sniffed her tail. Peaches licked Daisy's paw, which earned her a quick swat, but that didn't do much to rebuff the bold little dog. She licked her other paw in a sassy, "take that!" move. Ginger laughed.

Ginger reached for her phone again on the nightstand. She lay back against the mattress and angled her phone above her head, trying to get all three of them in the frame together. When she managed it, she snapped her fingers. Miraculously, Peaches and Daisy looked up at her phone, and she took the photo.

She rolled over to study her attempt at a selfie. With a little editing and cropping, it wasn't too bad.

Giggling, she sent it to Cal.

Beautiful, he replied seconds later.

They look happy, don't they? she responded.

Yep! Luckiest animals in the world right now, he sent back.

She spent the rest of the night rereading those words.

16

Best brown sugar latte I've ever tasted right here at Coffee Loft. I'm thinking everything on the menu is top tier. Thanks, CL, for the great experience! ~ J.D. Webby

Without Peaches and Ridley barking the night away, Cal focused on wrapping up a proposal for a client. That photo Ginger sent him of her, Peaches, and Daisy was a sweet distraction. He kept pulling it up on his phone to stare at it and smile. Later in bed, he brought the image up again as he lay there in the dark, with Ridley snuggled against his side. With her dark hair fanned out against her coverlet, and smiling so hard her eyes were little slits above her plump cheeks, Ginger was the most beautiful woman he'd ever seen. His chest ached thinking about her.

Then he crashed hard.

He awoke the next morning without the perpetual

headache that had plagued him the last few days. Coffee finally sounded good again.

He'd arranged the night before to pick up Peaches at Ginger's place before she headed into work. He prayed during the drive to Coffee Loft that dog sitting hadn't been too chaotic for Ginger, and that she was still speaking with him.

When he pulled into an empty parking spot a short time later, she wasn't standing at her apartment window above Coffee Loft, waiting for him. A good sign.

Standing at the door, Ginger looked like a sunny, fall morning personified. She smoothed the burnt-orange sweater on her trim figure with both hands before opening the door wider. His heart did a little stutter-step when she grinned at him. A *very* good sign.

"I love this dog," she gushed. "Did you know that she can balance a treat on her nose then snap it up mid-air?"

"Yeah? So, the sleep-over went well?" The Peaches-sized weight on his shoulders lifted.

"Daisy and Peaches *love* each other. I'm shocked," she said. She opened the door wider for him to enter.

He gazed around the sunny room and found Daisy and Peaches on opposite ends of a futon, basking in the sunshine coming through the front window. Coupled with the literal small forest of plants scattered about, the brightly patterned pillows, framed floral prints, and the pale green gauzy curtains undulating from an open window, the room radiated happiness. It was a tangible vision of what his heart felt like at the moment. The uncertainty surrounding the shelter, Ginger's willingness to help him with Peaches, and the news that the sleep over had gone smoothly made him feel... *something*.

"What's wrong?" Ginger asked.

He stood rooted to the spot, taking it all in. A lump rose in his throat, and the sensation was so odd, so out of character for him, that he almost turned around to leave so he could regain his bearings.

"Cal?"

Ginger's eyes held his with soft concern when he looked her way. She shifted and her hand reached for his forearm, but he grasped it instead on an impulse.

Seconds ticked by as she glanced down at their interlocked hands. Embers of desire steadily crawled up his arm and spread throughout his chest. It was near impossible to stand there, holding her hand, and not take a step forward. Her presence was a magnet to his iron-clad defenses. He'd fought his attraction to Ginger for so long that he'd grown accustomed to shrugging off her smiles and lingering looks as nothing more than a casual friendship. But this morning was different. His longing had finally worn away that armor.

What is she feeling? He wished he knew. She stood frozen, her gaze resting on their hands. He took a chance, his thumb grazing her knuckle.

Speak up before it's too late.

"Ginger, I—"

She slid her hand away from his as she turned toward the kitchen.

No!

"You're not feeling poorly again, are you? I have some more of that tea in my fridge already made, if you'd like some," she said over her shoulder. Ginger was already in her kitchen, peering into the open door. She pulled out a pitcher. "Here, I'm just going to send you home with some anyway." She talked fast like she tried to distance herself from their shared moment.

While Ginger flitted about the kitchen, opening cupboards, pouring tea, and rinsing the pitcher, he fought a potent urge to tell her how he felt.

But she'd pulled away. It was a clear signal she wasn't invested in the moment, unlike him. He was no Romeo, but even he could read the signs.

His phone buzzed in his pocket.

Charleen.

He hoped she was calling to say they'd fought off moving the deadline to vacate sooner than December.

He stepped out onto the stairwell landing to take Charleen's call, keeping an eye on Ginger. Ginger, in turn, cast furtive glances his way, too, while she bustled around the kitchen.

"Someone wants a meet-and-greet with Peaches," Charleen said as soon as Cal answered.

"That was quick. Didn't her profile just show up on the site last night?"

"I've been working behind the scenes, because I know this situation is tough on her," Charleen said.

He glanced at the couch where Peaches still lounged against an oversized pillow. Sunlight bathed her coat like warm butter. She shifted, exposing her belly as she rolled onto her back. One eye barely open, the dog didn't look to him like she was traumatized at the moment.

"Do you want to give them my contact info so I can set something up?"

"I'll do that," said Charleen.

He stepped back into Ginger's apartment after Charleen ended the call.

Ginger handed him a to-go cup of tea and Peaches' overnight bag, meeting his eyes, but she hurriedly glanced away. It was as if he'd merely imagined holding her hand a few minutes ago. The lingering sensation of their touch was the only hint that it had happened in the first place.

"Is everything okay?" she asked, her voice taut.

Peaches hopped off the couch and stretched, hunching like a cat, before she sauntered over to them. He scooped her up.

"That was Charleen, calling about Peaches."

Ginger's brows lifted. "Oh?"

"Someone wants to do a meet-and-greet this afternoon."

She looked at Peaches, nestled comfortably in his arms.

"That's...good news, right?" she asked, crossing her arms.

If he didn't know better, he'd swear Ginger's expression held a bit of regret.

17

offee Loft has certainly unleashed my taste for premium coffee. Step aside, Starbux. This shop around the corner is the only place worth their weight in beans. ~ Me & Boo

Her heart still beat like mad. She was afraid to look down in case it pulsated against her tee-shirt. And Cal needed to leave so she could think.

"Sure, it's good news," Cal said, stroking the dog's neck. Peaches' black eyes studied her through the tumbled mop of hair on her face. "The sooner she settles into her new forever home, the less trouble she'll have leaving my place."

Cal acted like he hadn't just taken her hand. It *was* a moment, wasn't it? What did it mean? And what had he been about to say before she panicked and escaped into the kitchen for his tea. She should ask him.

Or maybe not.

Cal set Peaches down again and gently pushed her into the carrier. He latched the door, hoisting it and juggling his tea at the same time. She'd opened the door for him, but he stayed put.

"I can carry the bag if that'll help." She held out a hand to take something.

Why wasn't he in a hurry to go?

And why was she in such a hurry to see him leave?

Wasn't this what all the fluttering in her chest was about? Cal and her. Together. She could deny it for all the beans in Bolivia, but that wouldn't change the fact that Cal had wormed his way into her heart.

He gave her a thin smile. "I've got it. Thanks for watching her. See you soon."

She leaned her forehead against the door as soon as she closed it. Her heart called out, "Don't go." But her head, the place where memories of hurt and rejection resided, argued against it. It was safer this way.

Flexing her hand, she almost could feel the tantalizing sensation of him taking hold of it within the confines of his own. *So strong and warm...*

She listened to Cal descend the stairs. He took three steps and hesitated.

Silence.

Holding her breath, she pressed an ear to the door.

Was he coming back? What was he thinking?

But then his footsteps echoed in the stairwell, growing more distant. Seconds later, the outside door clicked open and shut.

T houghts about the morning muddled her mind throughout the day as she, Merris, and Alice prepped for the extended hours of the Fall Days Festival the next day. Trying to get anything accomplished on a Friday was the challenge, though.

She and Alice sat at the longest table in sight of the front counter and assembled the hot chocolate packets as a give-away item. Alice had the prettiest handwriting, so Ginger asked her to sign the little Coffee Loft tags attached to the packets with "Love, your Coffee Loft Team."

"Ginger?"

She looked up to catch Alice staring at her.

"What is it?"

The young woman looked pointedly at the bag Ginger assembled. "I don't think you want to do that."

Ginger glanced at the bag that she'd closed with a foil twist tie. Inside, her store key was nestled amongst the hot chocolate packet, the mini marshmallows, and a chocolate-covered spoon.

"Goodness." She untied the bag to retrieve the key. "At least someone is paying attention. Thank you. I would have torn the store apart looking for it."

Alice gave her a one-sided smile as she concentrated on her own work. "You have a lot on your mind, I'm sure."

"What about you? Are you getting the hang of it here?" Alice was a diligent worker so far, but quiet. Her perpetually neutral expression made her hard to read. "Do you have any questions?"

"I love it here. I was worried about making the drinks. You know, remembering the different combinations and drink names, but it's easier than I thought." She shrugged. "I'm not as quick as I should be."

"It'll come in time. And look at the drink cards if you can't remember. I'd rather have a drink that's thoughtfully crafted, than a quick one that doesn't taste well. Don't sacrifice taste for time."

A small line had formed at the counter. She caught Merris's eye, silently asking if she needed help. With a slight shake of her head, Merris signaled that she could handle it.

Alice nodded. "Is there any chance I'll be able to take on more hours when, you know, I get better?"

Heading into the holiday season, business always picked up. They'd talked about Alice's work schedule at her interview, but it didn't sound like her other part-time job was flexible.

"Sure, but have the time constraints of your other job changed?"

Alice frowned as she concentrated on stuffing another baggie. "It could? I don't know, it's all such a struggle. I need something full-time, truthfully."

She'd hired Alice on a part-time basis. Merris worked close to full-time, but even her schedule had constraints. Ginger loved to accommodate when she could; she knew barista jobs were plentiful around the area.

"I just don't know how I'll get to where I want to be while I'm in my current situation."

Ginger tucked the last packet of hot chocolate into a bag, then closed it.

"Let me think on this some. I'm sure we'll find a solution to make you happy, at least temporarily."

Alice thanked her as her eyes shone with teary emotion. "Thank you. Merris said this place was amazing. I really want to soak up as much as I can, you know, so I learn everything there is to know about the coffee business."

Ginger carried the box loaded with the giveaway samples back to her office, stewing about Alice's situation. She set the box on her desk and picked up her phone to check for messages. It was an email notification that made her stop in her tracks.

From the Greenhaven Economic Council.

Her breath stuttered to a stop.

The Forty Under Forty Award. She didn't expect to hear for another week at least.

She eased herself into her chair, taking a deep breath.

D*ear Ms. Giatti:*
    Thank you for providing us with your portfolio for the Forty Under Forty Award. After careful consideration of the ninety-seven applications, we're pleased to inform you that you have been selected as one of the top five candidates. The honor of being short-listed—

S he pumped her fist. *Yesss!*
    And even if she didn't make it to the top spot, the two-thousand-dollar grant for second- through fifth-place finishers would help her expansion plan.

The first person she thought to share the news with was Cal.

She scrolled through her contacts until she came to his name.

And froze.

Three little letters. C-A-L.

So much weight attached to so small a name.

What would they say to each other after she told him the news and he congratulated her? There was so much to say, but she didn't know how to even begin. Not when what had happened yesterday stood between them like a two-ton elephant with heart emojis for eyes.

No, she'd wait to tell him the news. Her heart might be ready but it still had some reconciling to do with her head. *Thanks, Marco.*

She pressed a hand against her chest, her heart beating against her palm.

It was safest that way.

18

You'll think you died and went to coffee heaven once you taste Coffee Loft's lavender frappe. Pure delight!
~ R. Klybourne

Cal ambled up to the walk-up window at Coffee Loft late Saturday afternoon, hoping to get his café au lait without Ginger spotting him.

Yesterday morning had been a dream that went off the rails. He still wished for a do-over.

He'd cursed himself for the rest of the day, feeling the fool for taking her hand. His folly was only outshone by his hope that she'd call to finish what he'd started. Something like, *Cal, I can't stop thinking about you taking my hand. Wanna get together and try it again?*

Right.

He couldn't be more out of practice with this whole dating thing, not that they were dating. Far from it. The gala was a week away, and he needed to get a grip on himself. Seal the deal, so to speak. If he failed, he didn't foresee another chance to make Ginger see how right they were for each other.

At the window, he placed his order with Alice, the new employee. While she took his payment, Ginger scurried past the window inside, two mugs in hand.

His mouth went dry.

She did a double take, a smile lighting her face when she noticed him. She mouthed "wait" before she disappeared again.

Alice handed him his change, then he parked himself on a cedar bench in the brick-paved garden area to wait for his drink and Ginger. His mind whirled, trying to come up with something witty in case the awkwardness from yesterday remained.

"Hey there."

Ginger walked toward him, carrying his drink. She'd swept her dark hair into a high ponytail, though the ends still brushed her shoulders. Sun had kissed her nose and cheeks as if she'd spent time outside over the last day. It only enhanced the greenness of her eyes, and he swallowed hard. He couldn't imagine a time when the sight of her wouldn't make it hard to breathe.

"You have a busy night ahead of you." He made more room on the bench when she sat next to him.

"Are you coming? I figured it'd be a perfect time to bring Peaches." Her eyes grew large as she pressed a hand to her chest. "Wait, did she get adopted?"

"No. She didn't get along with the family's dog."

Ginger slumped. "Oh, thank goodness... I mean, I'm glad they found that out before they brought her home."

"We'll find her the right family eventually. For now, she's getting more content by the hour." Had Peaches worked her magic on Ginger during the sleepover? If he wasn't mistaken, Ginger seemed genuinely concerned about the little pooch.

Maybe this self-proclaimed cat person was making room in her heart to be a dog person, too. It'd be one more reason to adore her.

"Did I hear something recently about the shelter having to move?" she asked.

"It's true. There's a new sewer project going through the property. Charleen tried to stop it." He shook his head. "We have to find a new place by the end of the year, if not sooner."

"That's awful. Any leads?"

"Maybe? The board will know more soon."

She perked up. "Hey, good news. I got word that I've been short-listed to the top five in the Forty Under Forty."

"Congratulations. I didn't expect otherwise." He put up a hand, and she high-fived him.

"They'll announce the top candidate in a few weeks." She clasped her hands in her lap. "I get nervous just thinking about it."

"I don't think you have anything to worry about." He marveled that someone as accomplished as Ginger doubted herself.

Ginger toed the bricks, nodding. She was quiet for a moment, and he studied her to gauge her mood. Should he apologize for yesterday, or would that add another dose of awkwardness to the situation?

"So, will you come?" she asked again, keeping her attention on the ground.

"I'll come, but I'll leave the dogs at home. The crowd might be a little overwhelming for Peaches. And you know how Ridley acts in public. Everyone is his best friend."

She wore a wistful smile. "I'd really love your help."

"Yeah?"

"I need someone to man the hot chocolate bar. Merris and Alice will be busy behind the counter. Jace is out of town, but my newest hire will be working the kitchen, and I need to be peeking in on him quite a bit."

"I'm your guy then."

She was studying her shoes again, but the smile crinkled the skin at the corner of her eye.

"I like the sound of that," she said softly.

Maybe his ears were playing tricks on him. At least that's what he *thought* she'd said. Maybe yesterday's hand-holding episode had worked a little magic overnight.

"What time?"

She stood and brushed her hands together, grinning down at him. The back of his neck tingled.

"Five thirty. *Sharp.*"

───────

He took Ridley and Peaches for a quick walk around the park before he was due back at Coffee Loft. The sharp, sweet scent of wet cedar hung in the air after an afternoon drizzle. Now, an impressionist sunset was in the making. Gold and pink swaths painted the October sky, dappled with blue where the feathery clouds broke apart.

Ridley, probably sensing Cal's do-or-die desperation surrounding their new houseguest, toned down his enthusiasm around the much smaller dog. Watching Ridley with Peaches was a sight. He'd nose her head as he walked alongside her, as if he gently reminded her of his presence. Peaches, all business, held her nose high as her little legs did double-time to keep up with him and Ridley. She'd curl her lips if he got in her face for too long, but Cal had yet to see her nip. A good sign. Their yin-and-yang dynamic would eventually gel into a compatible one soon. It'd make it much easier to get a good night's rest, at least.

He changed at home, fed the dogs, then walked back to Coffee Loft, arriving five minutes earlier than Ginger's requested time. Tables had been moved to make room for an additional long table that she'd draped with a tablecloth when he walked up behind her. He lifted the silver urn he spotted on one of the nearby tables and set it down as soon as she smoothed the table cloth.

She glanced sideways at him, her eyes popping. "You made it."

Why wouldn't he? "Of course, I did. You asked."

"I know. But then I felt guilty after I'd asked. You've had a lot on your plate lately."

"I'm not so busy that I couldn't be here for your big night."

Ginger briefly touched his arm, sliding her hand down his sleeve. "You're almost at café au laits-for-life status," she teased. "Thank you."

He smiled so the tinge of disappointment wouldn't register on his face. Her doubt that he wouldn't come after she'd asked for help bothered him. Like she'd prepared herself to be let down. More fallout from a bad relationship like he'd suspected, no doubt.

Ginger gathered the wicker basket in her arms from the other table and set it next to the urn, then unloaded condiment jars, napkins, and a small hot chocolate bar sign.

He took the lid from one jar to peek inside. Sprinkles. Another jar held cookie crumbs. There were also chocolate chips, mini marshmallows, and cinnamon candies.

"Do you have chocolate-coated spoons?" He replaced the lid on the last jar.

Ginger nodded to the other table. "I do."

"Edible stir sticks?"

That drew a blank from her. "What do you mean?"

"Peppermint sticks or those waffle straws with the chocolate inside?"

She turned and put a hand on her hip, wearing a half-smile.

"Maybe I should have consulted you before tonight."

He chuckled. "I'm only a software guy."

"But it sounds like you've done this before," she said.

He smiled back, lifting a brow. "You could say I have a little experience."

She slowly shook her head. "How are you not taken?" she mused.

He felt his face grow warm as he held her gaze. "Maybe I haven't found anyone I want to get taken by yet."

Ginger's smile faded as they stared at each other.

"That's too bad," she answered softly.

There was no mistaking the subtle undertones of Ginger's words this time. If they weren't standing in the middle of Coffee Loft right now, with Alice and Merris within sight, he'd seriously consider seizing this moment. Or he could stop second-guessing himself, take her by the hand, and lead her into the back room for some privacy. Those parted, rosy-hued lips begged for—

Ginger let out a squeak when Merris popped in between them.

"Here, boss. What do you think?"

He almost leaned against the steel pole nearby, so intense was his desire to prolong the moment. Ginger must have felt it, too. She placed a hand against her cheek as the skin of her throat rippled. The smile she wore for Merris's sake was strained.

"It'll be hard to miss, which is exactly what we want, right, Cal?" she said as her voice cracked. She tossed her ponytail behind her shoulders as if resetting herself.

That snapped him back to earth. He focused on the painted box she took from Merris. Fall hues of green, gold, and orange would definitely grab attention if that was the goal. But then he noticed something about the lidded box with a cut-out on the top that made him pause—the faint paw prints stenciled in black scattered over the surface.

"It's perfect," Ginger raved. She placed it at the end of the hot chocolate station.

"Sidewalk traffic is picking up," Merris said. "I'd better check in with Alice and close the walk-up window."

"Yes, thanks. We'll have a hard enough time keeping the

counter customers moving if we don't." She fiddled with rearranging the jars and other items on the table to make room for the box.

He pointed to the box. "So, what's that for?"

She leaned against him, giving him a gentle nudge with her arm, and it took every ounce of concentration to make sense of what she said.

"It's for the shelter. I want to help." She took a standing frame from inside the box and handed it to him. "This explains about the shelter having to relocate. The box is for donations."

She'd taken the time to type up a flyer, explaining the dire situation at Hearts Fur Love. He read her plea for more volunteers and donations, ending with the contact info to help. His throat tightened as he noticed the photo she'd used. It was one of Charleen and him standing next to the shelter sign in front of the building. At his feet was Ridley. It was the first day he'd brought him home as a new foster.

Ginger cleared her throat. "I found that picture online. I hope that's okay to use. Maybe I should have asked first."

"This...it's very generous. Amazing, actually."

She faced him and stepped closer, close enough that he noticed how her lashes fanned out against her cheek and her irises were more teal than green. He gulped.

"You've really inspired me. Between watching you come to the patio with your dogs, and...and what you did for me after the storm...you've just made me think. I want to make an impact, too."

"But you have. I've told you that. Coffee Loft isn't just a place serving coffee. It's a refuge for a lot of people."

"I want to do more."

Ginger's gaze lingered on his face until her focus shifted from his eyes to his mouth as she tugged gently on her bottom lip with her teeth. Stars popped into his vision before he realized he held his breath or locked his knees or both. He let out a silent breath. He could almost feel her fingers caressing his face.

"You've done more than you realize."

"I want...more," she said again in a husky whisper.

Only this time he assumed she didn't mean donating to charity or volunteering or making a community impact in some way.

She wanted more of *them*.

Of *him*.

And he was here for it. Today, tomorrow, for however long she wanted him.

But then the bells above the front door jingled next to them, and the spell was broken.

19

When Gilbert's Java House closed last year, I thought I'd have to find a new place somewhere out of town. Then I found Coffee Loft, and it became my new favorite place. ∼ Frank Beck

Air. I need air.

Cal gazed down at her with a longing she could only describe as fierce.

Lightheaded, she took a deep breath.

"I need...to f-finish up here. It'll get busy in a matter of minutes."

She didn't wait for his reply as she cut through the shop toward her office. She bumped into her desk chair as she hurried to the back door, pushed it open, then leaned against it when it closed, gasping.

Ginger closed her eyes, tilting her face toward the darkening sky, willing her heart to slow so it wouldn't beat its way out of her chest.

Am I even ready for what I've started?

The image of Cal's eyes burning into hers flooded her senses with an intensity she'd never felt before. That desire still pulsed through her like a living thing, flowing into her feet and fingertips and to the ends of her hair. His presence filled her like water, quenching her thirst that had been denied for too long.

Dear Cal. She'd left him so quickly he was probably still frozen in place, wondering what happened.

She braced her hands on her knees, still waiting for her heart to regain its normal rhythm.

Ever since she'd interviewed Cal, she knew she was done for. He'd surprised her with his attentiveness and humor, his humble demeanor, and quiet, self-assured strength. She'd realized that her initial impression of him was her problem, not his.

He was decidedly *not* like Marco. Not in the least.

And with that newfound knowledge, she looked forward to his visits to Coffee Loft even more. She longed for his company. When he appeared on her patio, happiness spread through her like steamed milk on a latte.

But taking their friendship to the next level? That's what stopped her cold.

Fear of a repeat relationship like she'd had with Marco was to blame. The pain was still palpable at times, even though she'd convinced herself that she'd moved on in the thirteen years since the divorce. But, clearly, she hadn't; she'd just perfected her ability to bury the hurt. So, nurturing a romantic relationship hadn't mattered before now.

But Cal changed that. This one *was different.*

Squeaky brakes shook her out of the moment. Kit's battered pickup appeared around the corner of the alley and stopped in one of the parking spaces behind Coffee Loft. Her friend waved wildly through the windshield before she killed the engine.

"Special delivery," Kit crowed through the open side window. The door groaned in agony when she opened it. In her hands were three pastry boxes filled with cider donuts. The heavenly aroma permeated the air as Kit walked toward her.

"What are you doing out here all by your lonesome? Isn't the festival in full swing?"

"Yes. Just needed to catch my breath."

Kit looked perplexed. "Okay. Well, sorry I'm late. My last tour of the day ended on an unexpected note. Some yahoo on a speedboat took out my dock. I had to ask the casino if I could use theirs. That involved finding someone to shuttle me and my guests back to Port Chance."

"Oh, my. I'm so sorry." Kit didn't look the least bit ruffled. The woman had nerves of banded iron.

"Eh. A day in the life." She narrowed her eyes. "Are you sure you're alright?"

"I am." She straightened after realizing she still had her hands planted on her knees, and took the pastry boxes from Kit. "Just bracing myself for the rest of the night."

Kit nodded slowly like she wasn't buying it.

"So, I have a favor to ask." She balanced the boxes in one

hand while she fished the door key from her pocket. "I'm desperate."

Kit looked concerned as she held the opened door for her to go in first. "What do you need?"

"A dress."

Kit's frown was punctuated by the back door slamming behind them.

Back in the office, Ginger blinked as her eyesight adjusted to the dim lighting.

Kit stared for a few extra seconds. "What for?"

"I'm going to the Hearts Fur Love Gala next weekend, and I don't have anything to wear."

"The easiest solution for that is to not go in the first place. I wouldn't go anywhere if I was expected to wear a dress." Kit feigned a shudder.

"You didn't go to your prom or homecoming?" Kit had a habit of embellishing.

"That was almost two decades ago," Kit said. "Almost like another *life*. How am I supposed to remember?"

"So, that's a yes?"

"No, I didn't go," she said flatly.

"You've never worn a dress to a wedding? Weren't you a bridesmaid in your sister's wedding?" If Kit denied it, she'd catch her in a lie. She'd seen Rose Wendell's wedding photo in Kit's house. Kit was near the front of a very long line of bridesmaids wearing dresses.

Kit gave her a deadpan look. "No comment."

She led Kit out into the shop. They stopped at the pastry case to unload the donuts. A long line at the counter already snaked toward the door. Merris and Alice hustled behind the counter like a well-oiled, coffee-making machine. And in the corner near the front windows, stood Cal. Of course, a small group gathered around him while he laughed and chatted like the natural-born charmer that he was. She smiled to herself.

"Hearts Fur Love. *Waaiiittt,*" Kit purred. "Don't tell me you're going with Mr. Rescue himself."

"It's just a friendly date."

Kit gave her a wicked grin. "You said 'date.'"

Exasperated with Kit's line of relentless questioning, she sighed.

"Cal invited me to a fundraiser. It was a compromise when I asked to interview him. It kind of took off from there."

"I'll say."

"Like I said, we're only friends."

Kit rolled her eyes. "Uh huh."

20

What's not to love about a coffee shop which not only serves the best cold foam brews in the whole state of Iowa, but welcomes dogs onto the patio? We were traveling through town when we spotted this cute little café. It was a great respite for my hubby and me, as well as our two dogs. Thanks, Coffee Loft! ~ the Beerlman Clan

Two hours into his hot chocolate bar shift, Cal got a desperate call from Charlene. Someone who'd volunteered to walk dogs that night had a family emergency, and there was a no-show. *Can you come?* she'd asked.

He'd begged off of the last hour at Coffee Loft after he found Ginger in the kitchen, helping the new hire catch up on washing dishes.

"Of course, Cal. We've got it covered." Ginger dried her

soapy hands on a dish towel and faced him. "Thank you so much."

Unspoken words flowed between them as he looked down at her. She smiled.

"I'll see you soon, then?"

Ginger nodded as her smile broadened. A pink hue spread across her cheeks.

"You will."

With a full kennel, he and Charleen and one other last-minute volunteer managed to get the dogs exercised in just under two hours. It was a crazy jugglefest of moving dogs out of their kennels and into the larger outdoor pens, giving them as much recreation time as possible without the full roster of volunteers available.

When Cal hooked the leash onto the rack inside the shelter, having walked the last dog of the night, Charleen poked her head out of the office and summoned him.

"Just got this message from one of the board members," she said, looking at her phone. "The city wants us out of the building by the end of next month."

"*What*?! That's sooner than anyone expected."

"They want to demo this place before winter, so they can start work as early in the spring as possible." Charleen sighed. "I don't know where we're going to go, or how we'll afford what we need on such short notice."

"The gala couldn't come at a better time," he mused, his mind running through the logistics of relocating thirty kennels while causing the least amount of stress to the dogs as possible. But if there was one person who could do it, it was Charleen.

"Even with the proceeds from that, it'll be tight," she said.

"Whatever you need, I'm here." He could rearrange his work schedule to accommodate the other volunteers. They'd need everyone to step up. Everyone *and* their families for such a task.

Charleen leaned against her desk, crossing her arms. "I appreciate it, Cal. If you know of anyone with a building this size, let me know. Of course, we're looking for a bit of property with it, too."

"I've already put some feelers out around town." He rubbed the stubble underneath his chin, thinking about Ginger's efforts earlier tonight. "Did I tell you about what they're doing for us at Coffee Loft?"

"If you did, I've forgotten. My mind is mush with everything happening at once."

"My friend Ginger—"

"The woman I met at your house. With Peaches."

"Yes. She's soliciting donations tonight at the festival downtown for the shelter."

"That's wonderful. Bless her heart." Charleen slipped on her coat.

"You've been to Coffee Loft, right?" He stepped aside as she closed her office door behind her.

"Are you kidding? Their dirty chai lattes are to die for. I don't go as often as I'd like, though."

She walked down the hall ahead of him, shutting off lights. In the other room, the cacophony of barking had died down as it usually did this time of night as everyone settled onto their beds. Muted classical music played softly from the speakers, a soothing sound for the dogs.

As he walked to his car, he wondered if Ginger was still at Coffee Loft. He could swing by, and he would count himself lucky if he caught her still cleaning up. Maybe he'd offer to help. And maybe they'd pick up where they left off with the conversation that had almost struck him speechless before the interruption.

But when he drove by the shop a while later, it was dark. In the apartment above, a single light illuminated the drawn curtains of one window. He slowed, thought of parking for a while to sit and relive the events of the day in the peace and quiet, before he went home to the love fest which would greet him when he walked in the door.

Was Ginger in bed, reading? Or having a cup of tea on her couch, with one hand resting on her cat? Whatever she was doing, he could imagine her face, every smile line and lustrous wave in her hair. Someday soon he hoped that he wouldn't have to settle for just daydreams. Someday soon could be tomorrow or the next day.

With a sigh, he rolled up to the stop sign at the corner and pointed the car in the direction of home.

And silently said goodnight to the light in the window.

21

The only way this place could improve would be to offer coffee flights! ~ Café Connoisseur

Monday morning dawned bright and cool—a postcard-perfect October day. When Ginger came downstairs and opened the shop at six, the picturesque scene outside made her pause at the bottom of her staircase. An autumn kaleidoscope of colors had transformed the street overnight. More leaves had fallen, carpeting the sidewalk with an amber, orange, and scarlet blanket. Greenhaven's scarecrow contest had been in full swing all month, too. Now each unique entry from the residents and organizations added to the festive vibe of the season.

She unlocked the front door and breathed in the scent of beans and the subtleness of yesterday's pastry selection still lingering in the air. Her attention was drawn to the corner where she and Cal had stood two nights ago, sharing a moment that hadn't left her mind since they parted. Snippets of their conversation popped into her head.

I'll see you soon, then?

You will.

Can't wait.

He'd left her at Coffee Loft to help at the shelter. His confident swagger as he walked out the door left her giddy with anticipation, looking forward to seeing him again before he was even out of sight.

That's why she'd kept her eyes on the patio all morning, hoping he'd show. The word *distracted* didn't even do justice to her state of mind. She filled the milk pitcher with vanilla syrup, locked herself out of the office, and told Mr. Cavallari to have a good night at seven thirty in the morning. Merris and Alice would lose their minds and quit before the day was over if she didn't get her head in the right place.

"Have you seen Cal yet today?" she asked Alice when they stood side by side at the back counter working on a drink order. It was one o'clock already, and he had yet to show his face. Mondays were the only days she counted on him coming in. His visits during the rest of the week weren't as regular.

"Oh, he came by the walk-up window when you were in back signing for that delivery."

Disappointment tinged her good mood.

"He did? Did he ask to speak with me?"

"No, he didn't. Oh, but he said to give you this." She slipped a piece of paper from her pocket and handed it to Ginger.

She capped the cold brew and called out the name on the side of the cup, then unfolded the paper. She looked forward to Cal's sweet notes now almost as much as she hoped to see the guy himself.

Had to leave town. Talk later hopefully? C. This time he'd drawn a heart around his initial.

Amidst his harried, last-minute schedule, he'd taken the time to come to Coffee Loft and leave her this note. She smiled and hoped he'd make good on his promise to talk later.

"Ginger? When you get a minute, can we talk?" Alice asked.

"Of course." She prayed Alice wasn't quitting. Her calm demeanor tempered the chaos of the rushes, and she was a quick study. "When Merris gets back from her break, we'll head outside."

Since Alice approached her the first time about her work challenges, Ginger had wracked her brain for solutions to help. Offering her more hours or more money weren't options until it got closer to Christmas. Merris had seniority, so a raise for Alice meant a raise for Merris. That wasn't possible.

After Merris came back, Ginger led Alice out to the empty patio. She looked distressed.

"What's wrong, Alice? Talk to me."

"The boss at my other job offered me full-time hours. I really don't want to leave here, but the money is so tempting. That job doesn't have a future for me, though."

She sat against the back of her seat, folding her hands on the tabletop.

"What do you want, Alice? Really. You said you wanted a coffee truck to take to art fairs and concerts. But what are you doing in the short term to get there?" She knew what it was like to have a dream, and feeling overwhelmed about making it happen.

"Well," she said, twisting the end of her braid, "I'm working here."

She nodded. "A great start. If you quit here, though, how will that help?"

"It won't."

"Can I give you some advice?"

Alice nodded. "I'd love some."

"You need to learn the coffee business top to bottom first. Forget the truck for now. That's down the road after you learn what goes into a great cup of coffee. From growing beans to brewing."

"Okay."

"Have you looked into any kind of coffee education courses?"

"A little. There's one in North Carolina. My dad lives there..."

"Does southwestern Wisconsin sound a little closer to home?"

Alice nodded.

"It's where I learned most of what I know about coffee. I didn't have a mentor, so I had to figure it all out on my own. But you've got a leg up on me, because I'm always here for advice."

"Thank you," Alice said with a nod.

"There's a roastery there, but they also run an education program. Most of the classes are online, but there are three to four in-person classes a year in the two-year program."

"That sounds amazing."

"If you want, I can get a contact name for you if you have other questions."

"Is it...expensive?"

Of course, that was a concern since this conversation started because of her lack of funds in the first place.

"I'm not sure what tuition is now, but it was reasonable when I went through the program. Tell you what, why don't you look into the classes first and talk to my friend. Then we'll worry about the money afterward."

"Okay, but what if I took this other full-time job? Would I still be able to work part-time here?"

"Are you sure you can handle sixty-plus-hour work weeks? Plus classes?"

Alice gave her a resolute nod. "My mom works twelve-hour days. I don't have a boyfriend. Or even a pet."

Ginger laughed. Pets could monopolize a person's life if allowed, all right.

"I want to make this work," said Alice. "I'll let you know what I find out."

After Alice left her on the patio, Ginger's mind whirled with possibilities to help her. Alice's predicament was so similar to her own story. If someone had held her hand along the way, what a world of difference that would have made. She'd wasted so much time figuring things out on her own without direction from someone who'd already walked the path. After her divorce, all she'd known was that she wanted a coffee shop and didn't want to rely on anyone else for her well-being ever again. It'd been a frightening time in her life.

Her desire to help Alice gave way to another feeling, one

she'd felt after taking care of Peaches overnight for Cal—contentment. It was so much more satisfying to look outward instead of focusing on her own needs, problems, and insecurities.

If, by chance, she was chosen for the larger Forty Under Forty award, the prize money would go a long way toward expanding the business. Reinvesting in Coffee Loft was her goal, after all. Expanding with a mobile truck might be her answer for growing *and* helping Alice at the same time.

Now there's a thought.

———

That night, Ginger loaded the empty tea mug into the dishwasher and started the wash cycle. Daisy wound her body around Ginger's legs, reminding her that it was dinner time. After filling Daisy's dish with food, she settled once again at the counter, this time to finish paying bills.

Her phone chimed.

A text from Cal. She smiled. He'd made good on his word.

Cal: Did Alice give you my note today?

Ginger: She did. Thank you for giving me a heads up.

Cal: I had to make a quick trip out of town. Not happy about the last-minute timing, but hey, it pays the bills.

Ginger: Where are you?

Ginger pushed her paperwork aside and cupped her phone in both hands.

> Cal: New Jersey, the land of liberty and prosperity.
>
> Ginger: What's it like? I've never been.
>
> Cal: Well, I'm looking out the window right now. I see clouds, clouds, and more clouds. Oh, and a bird is sitting on the window ledge looking at me.
>
> Ginger: Either that, or he's admiring his own reflection. When will you be back?
>
> Cal: Hopefully sooner than Friday. It's hard to predict these types of jobs. What, do you miss me?

Her mouth went dry. She stared at his casual-but-loaded question. Her fingers typed a response, deleted it, typed something else, erased it. She finally settled on: You can't even imagine LOL.

She gritted her teeth, watching the little dots dance up and down as he typed his response.

> Cal: I can hear those words dripping with sarcasm, even without the LOL.

Fingers hovering above the keyboard again, she weighed her response. Her chest swelled with emotion. Sarcasm was her second language, but tonight she was speaking fluent honesty.

Ginger: Or maybe not.

Cal: Are you saying I have no imagination or you're not being sarcastic? Please clarify.

Ginger: The latter.

She worried when he didn't reply right away, that maybe she'd scared him away. But her fear was unfounded a minute later.

Cal: Don't make me get on the next available flight. Because I will.

A tingle of delight zinged through her. She giggled.

Ginger: Finish your job. I'll be here when you're done.

Cal: I'm going to hold you to that.

Ginger: Good night, Cal.

She placed her phone back onto the counter as a sweet effervescence churned within her chest. It wasn't like her to wish the days away, but the gala on Saturday couldn't come soon enough.

22

*L*ove *this little place. Super friendly staff and the coffee is the absolute best I've had. Highly recommend!* ~ Tristin G.

The week passed in a blur after a long-time client's company suffered a major security breach. Cal had caught an afternoon flight to Newark after arranging for Charleen's college-aged son to stay at his house to dog sit Ridley and Peaches. He thought of asking Ginger to watch Peaches again, but after her crazy weekend organizing for the Fall Days Festival, he hated to take advantage.

It was a harried time out East. Delayed flights, a lost rental car reservation, and his credit card being compromised marked the four days and nights he spent in a room overlooking the Passaic River. He'd never been so happy to see the flat, burnished-gold fields of eastern Iowa when he touched down in Cedar Rapids on Friday.

Now, Cal tugged the bottom of his tie, trying to adjust its length without having to redo the thing for the tenth time. He appraised himself in the bathroom mirror and made a face. Good enough.

Behind him on the bed, Ridley and Peaches lay in identical positions. His five days away only seemed to have affected their appetites. Upon arriving home, Cal noticed Ridley nudging the treat cabinet throughout the day. Peaches had picked up Ridley's habit, too. Their entitlement for endless rewards seemed to be punishment for Cal leaving them.

On their bellies, faces between their paws, the dogs watched his antics as he readied himself for the gala. He'd spent most of the afternoon trying to wrap up writing a report. *Trying* was the key word. All he could think about was the night ahead with Ginger.

Tonight is it.

But with only a handful of meaningful conversations and a few loaded looks over the last month, was it enough to finally break all the way through Ginger's protective façade? A friendship years in the making, and it was all coming down to a three-hour window at a shelter charity function.

He'd apologized for leaving her in the dark for a few days. The week had truly been a nightmare, with zero time for leisure after he and Ginger had texted late Monday night. He'd literally left his hotel at six every morning, only to return at eight in the evening, sometimes nine, with a cold sub and bag of chips he'd grabbed from the deli in the lobby. A half-eaten sandwich left on the nightstand the next morning was the only proof he'd eaten something before he collapsed into bed. It sounded like an excuse as he explained the week to her. He didn't blame her for feeling left out.

D id you have an easy flight back home? she'd asked when he checked in that morning to make arrangements for the gala.

> Cal: I suppose. I would have rather not left Greenhaven in the first place.
>
> Ginger: Oh, yeah? Why not?
>
> Cal: Hmmm, let me think. There's this woman who owns Coffee Loft. I can't stop thinking about her.
>
> Ginger: I bet she knows what you're going through.
>
> Cal: Maybe we should meet to commiserate.
>
> Ginger: How's tonight?

Their exchange left him whistling all the way on his trip around the park with the dogs.

Still in front of the mirror, he slipped his fingers into the space between the collar and his neck, tugged at the fabric some more, then turned off the bathroom light.

No room to breathe.

Movement outside made him pause as he reached for his jacket across the back of the chair.

Or maybe it was the woman in the car who'd just pulled

into his driveway. It wouldn't be the first time she affected his oxygen level.

He hoped tonight wouldn't be the last, either.

23

sweet gem of a coffee shop right here in Greenhaven! Try this place ASAP. You won't be disappointed. ∼ Friday morning gals

With nerves as taut as guitar strings, Ginger walked up to Cal's front door, careful not to catch a heel in the brick walkway. A potent mixture of anticipation and dread had almost paralyzed her on the drive over.

It's just Cal.

The whole process of getting ready for tonight—dress alterations, hair appointment, getting her nails done—was a constant reminder of what caused her angst in the first place. She might know no one at the gala, and instead have to make small talk, which sent her anxiety to a whole new level.

Something had happened between her and Cal at the Fall Days Festival, but the week away from him seemed like a mental reset. She fretted about if treading the already blurred line of their relationship was the right choice. Her thoughts brewed together into one perfect, emotional storm.

It's just Cal. It'd become her mantra throughout the day, to no avail.

Her fist was poised to knock when the door opened.

Cal, looking every bit the ideal guy in her daydreams, stepped aside to let her in. Ridley and Peaches immediately surrounded her, coming from out of nowhere. Despite the four paws and two mouths vying for her attention, she couldn't take her eyes off of Cal.

He wore dark dress slacks that looked like they'd been sewn on him. The berry-hued shirt couldn't have brought forth the blueness of his eyes any more. And the tie, well, she loved the mosaic pattern, but it skewed a little to the left, like he'd tried pulling it into place. Or maybe she'd interrupted a little tug-of-war between him and Ridley.

"You look—"

The compliment was interrupted by Cal's dogs, who acted like she'd bathed in beef drippings. And Cal wasn't any help. He stood frozen, still looking at her like she'd just disembarked from an alien ship.

"Help, please?"

She held Ridley's paws like they were ready to waltz. Meanwhile, she was pretty sure Peaches was tasting the shaving lotion on her leg and liking it.

Her desperate tone must have registered because Cal took over the dance with Ridley and gently shooed Peaches away with his foot.

"I'm so sorry," he gushed. "It's just...you look absolutely *stunning*."

She shook out a tissue from the packet in her purse and dabbed the saliva from her calf. Aside from being coated with dog drool, his compliment set off a rhythmic beat of quivers in her chest.

"Thank you." She stayed focused on wiping her leg, so he couldn't see her complexion giving a winning representation of a Ruby Red grapefruit.

He held out his hand.

She gasped and straightened, her eyes darting from his hand, to his face, then back to his hand. First the compliment, now...now *what*? Would he pull her into an embrace? Did he want to kiss her? The night was moving way too fast. At least that's what the warning voice in her head told her. But, since when did she heed anything that it advised? She casually slipped her hand into his. The pulsations in her heart tapped out a love melody that—

"I, uh, was going to take your tissue," Cal said as the skin on his throat rippled.

She jumped like she'd been scalded, pulling her hand away.

Oh, the humiliation.

It was like junior high all over again, full of end-of-the-world mix-ups and embarrassing catastrophes.

His expression was a comical mix of shock, discomfort, and something bordering on what she could only describe as lovesickness. He probably mirrored the emotions playing across her face at the moment.

It was going to be a long night.

———

They finally made it to Cal's car after the dogs settled into their respective crates and Cal fixed his wonky tie. As they drove, he explained that the historic hotel in downtown Bedden was the site chosen every year to host the Hearts Fur Love annual gala. One of the managers also volunteered at the shelter and was able to get the top floor ballroom at a steep discount for the event. Ginger had visited the restaurant adjacent to the lobby on occasion—an elegantly restored space in itself with dark mahogany paneling, crimson carpets, and stained-glass transoms topping the enormous windows facing the sidewalk. She'd never seen the ballroom, though.

She and Cal stepped into the elevator. He pressed the button for the twenty-eighth floor. They were alone when the doors shut.

"I talked to my new employee about starting her own coffee business." It was the first topic that popped into her head as she tried to come up with something to fill the silent ride to the top floor.

He backed up against the wall and gave her a sidelong glance.

"Oh, yeah? Does she have what it takes to run her own shop?"

"Well, her goal is a little more unconventional. She wants a *mobile* coffee business."

Cal eyed the floor number as it ticked upward. "Those trucks are pretty popular if you park them in the right place."

She laughed at Cal's simplified version.

"I told her it's a lot more complicated than 'parking it in the right place.'"

Cal shot her his movie star grin. "You know what I mean. You've mentioned acquiring a truck before if I'm remembering right."

"It's been on my mind for a while. Anyway, I'm mulling over the possibilities. I really want to help her."

"You're turning into a full-time philanthropist."

She looked at him to gauge if he was poking fun at her.

"What do you mean?"

"Inviting dogs for sleepovers, collecting donations for the shelter, and now taking Alice under your wing. It's pretty awesome."

"I just want to do my part."

He turned toward her so that his shoulder pressed against the back wall. His face was inches away. "And you're appreciated. Has anyone told you that lately?" he said in a soft voice.

"Yes, but I don't mind hearing it again."

She brushed his hand. His finger hooked hers, and they rode the rest of the way like that until the elevator lurched to a stop. Reluctantly, she let go of his finger as the music's tempo that greeted them as the doors slid open matched the thudding of her heart.

They stepped into a large, mirrored foyer. From there, the double staircase in front of them ascended to the ballroom. Three chandeliers the size of small, economy cars hung from the soaring ceiling, and she found herself marveling with an open mouth at the opulence of the room.

Charleen stood at the welcome table, handing them their name tags as they approached.

"Ginger, thanks so much for coming tonight." She gave

Cal an astonished look. "Has anyone seen my friend Cal Donner?"

"You know I'd rather have come in jeans and a tee. Don't rub it in," he answered with a laugh.

They moved away from the table and toward the stairs, stopping to put on their name tags. She pressed it onto her dress, then did the same for Cal. Her hand lingered on his chest as she smoothed the tag onto his dress shirt. She looked up at him, and his lips were *so close*.

"Thank you," he murmured as his gaze caressed her

She nodded, taking a small gulp of air. "You're welcome."

"You have a lot of people to meet tonight. We'd better get started," he said.

"I'm not so good at this."

"I'll be right next to you." His sympathetic smile almost chased away her anxiety.

Cal's hand on the small of her back was like a balm as he guided her throughout the room, introducing her to a dizzying number of people. It stayed there as a constant comfort as she made polite conversation. Its warmth penetrated the fabric to soothe her frayed nerves. To her surprise, most people at least knew her as the face of Coffee Loft, but many also knew her by name. Cal stood silently at her side with a knowing smile as these new acquaintances gushed on about her shop.

The string quintet played throughout the cocktail hour as people filled out the silent auction cards, mingled, and sampled the platters of beef Wellington, crab rangoon, and stuffed mushroom appetizers that circulated the room. At one point, the musicians stopped for a brief break. When they started up again, Cal clasped her hand.

"Will you dance with me?" he asked.

She nodded. All she thought about as he led her across the room to the dance floor was how impossible it would be to speak with her body pressed against his for a song or two.

Cal turned back to her when they found an empty spot amongst the other couples. Folding his arm around her back as he took her other hand in his, she felt like she was floating.

"I'm going to apologize in advance for stepping on your toes since there's a high probability that it might happen," he said in her ear as the strains of the violin rose against the hum of conversation around them. His eyes blazed as he pulled back to look at her when she didn't answer right away.

"And I'll accept your apology if I can offer one of my own."

"Which is?"

"I wore the highest, most uncomfortable heels in my closet so I'd have an excuse not to dance tonight."

"How's that working out?" His one-sided grin couldn't make him any more irresistible.

"Completely failed."

"Lucky me," he whispered, as a shiver rippled the skin on her bare arms when his lip accidentally brushed her ear lobe.

If the night stretched on forever, she wouldn't mind at all.

24

We recently visited Coffee Loft, and I'm being completely honest here: it's the best coffee I've ever tasted. The espresso, and chai, and chocolate chip caramel frappe were truly delightful—some of the best I've ever tasted. The employees knew their coffee, which was impressive. The shop has a great ambience, too. Loved the mug wall and the eclectic seating. I wished I lived closer. ～ Bean Lover

Cal drove them back to his house with the windows open at Ginger's request. She pulled some pins from her hair that had kept it partially up for the gala, and now it flowed around her shoulders in the wind.

As she searched for music on his radio, he glanced at her off and on while they drove through the downtown traffic. Her profile was lit by the dashboard, and she frowned every time a song came on that wasn't her taste. When she passed by a hip-hop song and shook her head vehemently, he let out a chuckle.

"What?" she asked, keeping her eyes on the radio.

"Nothing at all. You're just too beautiful not to look at."

Her finger hovered in front of the screen, but then she gathered her hands in her lap as she slowly leaned against the seat, staring straight ahead.

The music coming from the speakers was a popular Stones song. He couldn't even name it now, not with what he'd just blurted. It popped out without him giving it any forethought, like it was the most natural thing in the world to share. He'd always been pretty free with giving compliments, but sometimes they missed the mark. It seemed like this one had fallen into the latter category.

He shifted in his seat as he pulled beside her car in his driveway a short time later. Turning off the car, he faced her.

"I'm sorry. That was… I didn't mean to make you feel uncomfortable."

"I'm not. It was…unexpected, is all," she said in a soft voice.

"Okay. But you'd tell me if I was out of line?"

She nodded as she looked at him, her eyes looming large.

"Thank you," she whispered. "No one has said that to me before. Not out of the blue like that."

He found that hard to believe.

Maybe Ginger sensed his skepticism.

"It's been a while since I've let a relationship, I mean… whatever we're——"

He smiled at her self-effacing demeanor. "I know what you mean."

"Let it get this far," she finished. She glanced out her window for a few long seconds before she turned back to him. "My ex-husband wasn't the greatest at giving praise. Criticism, on the other hand..."

This time when he took her hand, caressing the back of it with his other one, she didn't pull away. She'd never shared anything about her ex-husband. This was the first time she'd mentioned even being married before.

"The divorce was long ago. I've put it behind me. For the most part..." She made a face as her voice trailed off.

He listened with a nod to go on.

"But I've realized in the last month that I still have work to do."

"Do you still talk to him? Did you have kids?"

She shook her head. The dim lighting inside the car reflected a moistness welling in her eyes. "Thank goodness."

He hadn't realized he'd tensed his shoulders until she answered. It was sweet relief for a concern he didn't know he had until now.

"I shouldn't have burdened you with this, not after tonight."

He squeezed her hand. "You didn't. I want you to feel free to talk to me anytime. About anything."

"We had fun tonight, didn't we?" she asked. She rubbed the corner of her eye with one finger.

"We did. I'm glad you decided to come." He paused and swallowed, praying she didn't get the wrong idea about the next question. He just didn't want the night to end. "Do you want to come in for a bit? I make a killer spicy hot chocolate."

When she hesitated, he held his breath.

"Spicy, huh? I'm intrigued." Her smile lit up the dark interior. "But I do have an early day tomorrow."

Perfect. She'd drawn her own boundary. That was even better.

"I'll whip some up while you visit with the doggos, then you can be on your way."

Inside, he let Ridley and Peaches out into the backyard after they'd given him and Ginger a proper greeting, then he rummaged through his cabinet for his cocoa container and spices. In the other room, Ginger stood in front of the wall with framed photos of his family and vacations, sometimes stepping forward for closer examination.

"You've been to Banff? I so want to go," she said a few minutes later. The skiing trip he took two years ago must have caught her attention.

"It's beautiful. But only if you don't mind the cold." He brought her the hot chocolate and they sat on the couch. He nudged his opened laptop with his foot as he leaned back, resting both feet on the coffee table.

"I love winter," she said.

She blew over the top of her mug, took a sip, and her eyes lit up.

"Oh my gosh, Cal. This is delicious. Is it a secret recipe?"

"Not really. Found it online somewhere." He pointed to his mouth. "You have a little chocolate..."

Ginger touched her mouth, then an easy, slow grin spread across her lips, as if something had dawned on her.

"Remember when I said that to you? At Coffee Loft? You had a foam mustache."

He nodded at the memory. "You said you wouldn't wipe my mouth unless I was under five years old."

Ginger shook her head slowly, fighting a grin. She didn't look away this time when they locked eyes.

"But...there are other ways to take care of that," she said. Her gaze floated to his mouth. Her intake of breath wavered.

"Oh, yeah?" He stroked her cheek with his knuckles, and she closed her eyes with the same contented smile.

They sat that way for a while; he had no idea how much time had passed. Being near her was enough, and he didn't want to risk undoing the moment. His heart close to bursting, he promised himself if he was lucky enough for her to choose him, he'd never let a day go by when he didn't tell her how much he cherished her, appreciated her. *Loved* her.

Ginger opened her eyes to see him staring at her. Her hand reached up to cup his cheek and pull him closer. Slowly, he lowered his mouth to hers. A little gasp escaped her when their lips met. He smiled against her mouth as he pulled her against him and sank into the bliss of their first kiss, touching, tasting, and reveling in the delight of finally, *finally* feeling his dream come to life.

Something scratched the patio door.

Ginger's fingers grazed the back of his neck and tangled themselves into his hair. She pulled him deeper into the kiss.

Another scratch, this time more urgent.

His arm encircled her back, drawing her to him so that it seemed their bodies melded together like—

A long, mournful howl carried in from the patio.

Ginger pulled away. "What on earth?"

No, no, no, no.

"It's Ridley." Leave it to the big oaf to ruin the moment. He tried to prolong their kiss, but when he tried kissing her again, his mouth landed on the side of her nose when she glanced toward the patio.

Ridley yowled again, and it was immediately joined by a higher-pitched whine, perfectly in tune.

"Isn't that sweet? They're serenading us," she said.

"Or something," he said, pushing off the couch. "Probably just reminding me it's well past their snack time."

Ridley was about to experience the true meaning of being in the doghouse.

25

A midwestern coffee shop gem. ∼ R & P

No amount of deep breathing could slow the frantic beating inside her chest. A perfect night at the gala had just culminated in the most perfect kiss. During all of her wildest daydreaming, she couldn't have imagined one so delicious.

"I'll just be a minute," Cal said over his shoulder. "Peaches decided she doesn't want to come in after all. She plays this game all the time, trying to draw me outside so I have to chase her."

She sighed. His back to her, she admired the way his broad shoulders stretched his dress shirt to its limit. To think she'd just been snuggled up against him. "Looks like it works." She giggled as Cal disappeared outside.

Leaning forward to take another sip of her hot chocolate, her grip on the handle faltered. A bit of the drink sloshed over the side of the mug and onto the coffee table.

Wonderful.

She hurried to the kitchen to find paper towels before the liquid dripped onto the floor. Grabbing a handful, she sopped up the mess, then lifted Cal's laptop when she noticed a little puddle running underneath.

His screen came to life.

A document appeared like he'd been in the middle of working on something. She didn't mean to read it—she wasn't a snooper—but one line caught her eye, and then she couldn't *not* look.

I'm a friendly, energetic male with a sense of adventure...

Outside, Cal's faint outline ran after a little white missile in the backyard, assuring her that he was preoccupied. So, she read a little more:

...I'm not picky when it comes to cuisine; I'm definitely a foodie...
...if hiking is your thing, I'm up for it, or snuggling at home is always at the top of my list, too...
...let's get together and see if we can make this work...

A white-hot blaze of confusion coursed through her. Was Cal active on a *dating* site?

Peaches scurried through the door, followed by Ridley. They circled around each other near the kitchen—a frantic mixture of nails clicking on the ceramic tile and excited snuffing—until Cal came inside, closed the patio door, then set a treat box on the counter.

Ginger stood, her head swimming.

"Do you want me to top off your drink? I have a little left," Cal asked, tossing a treat into the air for Ridley, then another for Peaches.

An excuse to leave is what she really needed, time to think this through. If he asked her what was wrong, she couldn't explain what she'd just discovered without also calling attention to having had no business looking in the first place.

"Maybe I'll take this to go. It's late." She gathered up the soaked towels and her mug, and brought them to the kitchen. The taste of Cal's delicious hot chocolate left a bitterness on her tongue now. She glanced at him in time to catch the smile falling from his face.

"Oh, okay." Cal's brows dipped. "Is something...wrong?"

"Just have an early day tomorrow, like I said." She found the garbage can, tossed the towels, and set her mug on the counter. Her coat lay over the bar stool, so she shrugged it on, careful to avoid his gaze.

Cal pulled the top from a lidded cup and filled it with her hot chocolate.

"You can keep this." He gave her a sheepish smile. "I give them out when I have a booth at conventions."

"Thanks." She clamped her lips together, still feeling the sweet warmth of his mouth on hers. *But, that profile...*

"Let me walk you out," he said, walking around the counter, but she put up her hand to stop him. If he tried to kiss her again, she'd be forced to turn him down, to explain why she was upset. And she couldn't bear that.

"It's fine. Don't trouble yourself," she said over her shoulder. Her hand was already on the doorknob.

"Are you sure nothing's wrong?" he asked again.

She took a deep breath and turned toward him.

"It's just time for me to go. This"—she waved her hand to encompass the room, the laptop, *him*—"might not be the best idea."

"Ginger. What does that mean?"

The night air cooled her face when she opened the door. Her breath hitched as she fought the urge to close the door without responding. She inhaled, straining to keep her voice from wavering.

"It means it's late and I'm tired." She shrugged. Too much had been said already.

"*Ginger.*"

She fought the tears threatening to spill until she was safely cocooned in her car. When they started flowing, blurring her vision as she pulled out of his driveway, she drove slowly until she was a few blocks away, then parked at the curb and shut off the car.

Her hands still clutched the wheel, and she rested her forehead against it and sobbed.

She'd finally let her guard down. After years of living within the airtight walls she'd built around herself, sealing the cracks when the tiniest threads of daylight tried to filter in, she'd finally thrown open the windows and breathed. Cal had knocked, and she'd answered. He was the perfect antidote to her love-hardened heart.

An oncoming car passed, its headlights washing over her. She kept her head down but swiped at the tears wetting her cheeks. She despised this show of weakness in herself, and knowing that the insecurities she thought she'd dealt with long ago still could cause so much pain.

But now her defenses were down, and look where that had led.

26

From their wide-ranging choices of drinks, to the sweet little groupings for seating, this coffee shop ticks all the boxes for me. Well done, Coffee Loft! My new favorite spot. ~ Hilary C.

Cal stared at the closed door for a few moments, wondering how the night had come to such a screeching halt. Her hasty departure cut into him like an open wound. He pressed a hand to his chest as if tangible proof was right there, underneath his shirt, a slice on his skin. It couldn't have gone any better, from the moment she stepped into his house in that dress until Ridley and Peaches started pawing at the patio door. And it couldn't have ended any worse.

He shot the dogs a look even though they were blissfully unaware, already asleep on their respective dog beds.

What happened?

Picking up her cup, he traced the faint print of her lips on the rim.

That kiss.

He closed his eyes, trying to revisit the feeling that burned in his chest when she'd pressed against him, fingers combing his hair, her breath tickling his cheek. But the confusing turn of events kept him from pondering its delightful effects for long.

He breathed deeply as he set her mug into the sink, then crossed the room to the couch and sank into it.

He'd wait a few minutes for her to get home and then call. There had to be something he'd missed. Across the room, Ridley let out a groan as if he felt Cal's despair.

The dog adoption profile was lit up on his laptop screen. He'd been working on this one before the gala. Three more needed to be posted on the website by tomorrow night.

That's funny. He squinted at the document.

The screen had popped back to life without him touching it.

He stared blankly at the keyboard, wondering how—

Wait a minute—oh no.

He leaned in to reread what he'd been working on earlier in the day.

I'm a happy-go-lucky handsome guy if you're into the big, rugged types. I have a calm disposition with a sense of humor (I'll love to make you laugh!), but getting together with friends is just as fun...

That couldn't be what made her cut the night short.

But he bet it totally was.

He nodded as he read it again, this time trying to see it from Ginger's perspective.

Now he was certain. She'd practically run from his house tonight because of what she'd seen on his laptop.

Ginger thought he was trolling for dates.

The more the realization sank in, the more he understood. He buried his face in his hands. The timing was awful, especially since she'd just shared with him the history of her horrible marriage.

Scrambling for his phone, he found her name in his contacts.

His heartbeat kept time with the ringing of her phone. He was about to give up until the sounds of a connection made him sit up.

Thank you.

They'd clear this up in no time. A little misunderstanding is all.

But his call had only gone to voicemail.

27

*C*hai love you lots, *Coffee Loft!* ∼ The Harris Group

After a sleepless night, Ginger spent the morning downstairs in the shop even though she typically took Sundays off—her one sacred day during the week. Keeping busy was the only way she'd get through it without wallowing in uncertainty and fear.

It'd also keep her from answering the phone. Cal had called at least a dozen times. She didn't trust herself to sound reasonable and in control if she asked him about what she'd seen on his laptop. She hated confrontations. She'd finally texted him that she needed some time. His simple "okay" was somehow more heart-wrenching than witnessing the pain on his face when she'd left his house.

While she restocked the pastry case with a fresh batch of

blueberry-almond scones, Alice bounced up to her as she tied a Coffee Loft apron around her waist, ready to start her shift.

"So, I did some research on that school in Wisconsin you told me about. The guy I reached out to on Friday called me yesterday afternoon." She finished tying her apron, then swept her hair into a quick ponytail. "I'm going to run up there for a tour and an interview on my day off. You know, to see if it's doable. We'll also talk about financial aid." Alice talked fast and said more in less than a minute than she'd uttered since she was hired.

"That's wonderful. I'm happy to hear you followed through." It wasn't too hard to muster enthusiasm for Alice. She deserved it for taking the initiative. "I'm sure you'll find that it's exactly what you're looking for."

"And the best part is they offer scholarships and paid training on the days I would go up there for the hands-on portion of the classes."

Ginger closed the case. "And you're good with scheduling your schooling around still working here?" She'd been pondering the mobile truck idea for a while, but Alice's plight had hastened her decision to move forward with finding a truck. It would be the perfect training ground for her employees, present and future.

Alice offered to take the empty pan from her. "I want to, yes."

"Perfect. I'm sure everything will fall into place."

Merris hurried behind the counter, balancing a plastic bin filled with dirty mugs and dishes. Her flushed face was the effect of the unusually warm day.

"What will fall into place? What am I missing?" she asked.

Alice's normally neutral expression was all sunshine and smiles now. "I'm taking a coffee education course that Ginger recommended," she said.

Merris rested the tub against the counter. "I know someone who took one of those. She was really happy with it. Now she has her own shop."

Ginger nudged Alice's arm. "See?"

Merris zeroed in on her. "Cal's hanging out on the side patio by the walk-up window. Didn't know if you saw him," she said, wiggling her eyebrows.

"Oh?" She looked down at the plastic tub so Merris wouldn't see the shadow that had surely settled on her face at the mention of his name.

Truthfully, she'd made a point of not watching for him. Interacting with Cal when she was still discombobulated about last night wouldn't do either of them any good.

"What, you're not going to go flirt with him?" Merris prodded.

She let out an exasperated sigh as Alice left to take an order. She lowered her voice. "I don't flirt with the customers."

Merris squinted at her. "He's back to being a customer? What happened?"

"When was he not a customer?"

Merris's deadpan look called her bluff.

"Okay, what would you do if you found out the person you've been casually seeing wrote a new profile for a dating site?" Ginger hefted the dish bin from the counter with the intention of taking it to the kitchen to wash them herself. If he happened to come in looking for her, she'd be out of sight and up to her elbows in soapy water.

"While you're still seeing each other?" Merris asked. "That's just wrong, unless there was a mutual understanding."

Ginger shook her head. "There wasn't."

Merris frowned. "So, if it were me, that guy would be toast." She crossed her arms. "Wait, so this is about Cal?"

"*Shush.* I don't want anyone to hear. Yes, Cal."

"So, he *is* more than a customer," Merris said.

She chewed on her lip. "I should just let it go."

"You absolutely shouldn't let it go. He needs to be called out if it's true." Merris glared toward the front window. "Want me to talk to him?"

Ginger chuckled in spite of her mood. She could imagine Merris rolling up her sleeves and giving Cal a piece of her mind.

"Not necessary. I'll figure this out on my own."

Sweet moments from last night had replayed in her head all throughout the morning. It just didn't make sense. Their eyes locking when he led her by the hand to the dance floor. His mouth dropping open when he'd seen her in the dress. She could still hear the cadence of his tone when he'd uttered, "You're stunning." And she shivered every single time those words echoed in her mind.

But their relationship wasn't defined by only a single night. It'd been a slow awakening ever since the interview. She'd discovered she and Cal had more in common than she first dared to imagine: their shared love of old cars, music festivals, and Midwestern sunsets over the Mississippi. Business owners. Oldest of three siblings. Both had summer birthdays—hers fell on the first day of summer, his on the last.

She'd fallen for him. *Hard.*

Yes, she was ready to admit it, even though it pained her to think she might have already lost him.

A little while later, she left the kitchen and stopped in her tracks behind the front counter. Cal had moved from the shady side patio to the one by the sidewalk.

"What's he still doing here?" she said to no one in particular.

At the mug wall, Merris rolled her eyes. "Maybe he needs a break from the pooches. Or maybe he burned something on his stove and he's waiting for the smoky smell to leave his house. Or maybe"—she wiggled his personal cat mug in Ginger's direction— "it's a two-mug kind of day."

Exasperated, Ginger held out her hand.

"Give me that."

She walked over to the back counter to make his café au lait.

Espresso, scalded milk—nothing complicated, just like Cal.

She swallowed as the doubts crept forward again.

Coffee maker, coffee drinker. Was it all they were destined to be?

It is if you don't explain yourself.

She studied the minuscule bubbles on the creamy surface. Her hand hovered over the container of plastic stencils until she chose one. Her pulse skipped as she sprinkled cinnamon over it.

Either talk to the man or don't, but skip the subtle drink message this time.

She pushed away the thought. It's just a heart-shaped sprinkle of cinnamon, for goodness' sake, not a declaration of love.

You think he betrayed you.

But Cal is different. It just doesn't make sense. She looked down at the heart floating on the surface. Her feelings for him were still intact. But a painful, burning doubt was, too.

Merris moved in next to her to start another drink. She eyed the design, glanced at Ginger, then looked down at the mug again.

"So you're giving him the benefit of the doubt?"

She lifted a shoulder. "You don't think I should?"

Merris turned to face her and gripped her shoulders.

"Ginger, just talk to him. You're not making a life commitment here." She gave her a little shake.

"The heart's not too much?"

Merris snorted. "If that were the case, I've been hitting on people pretty much every day since I started here."

Ginger chuckled.

"But," Merris continued, "you shouldn't rely on coffee to do the talking forever. Tell him how you feel." She pressed her lips together and gave her a firm nod.

She pushed the mug toward Merris. "Can you take this to him, please?"

Merris gave her a sympathetic smile. "It'd mean more coming from you."

She sighed deeply and shook her head. "I can't. Not yet."

After delivering an iced coffee to another customer, Merris made her way to the patio. Cal, hunkered in front of his laptop, looked up when she set the mug next to him. His attention was drawn to the laptop again as soon as Merris left his table.

Cal didn't even notice her handiwork.

Look at your mug.

Merris returned, leaning against the counter with arms crossed, watching Cal.

"It's going to fade before he notices," Merris said.

"No worries."

"You're the most passive suitor." Merris pushed away from the counter. "I don't have the energy for this."

"Not suitor. Suitor*ess*." She stared so hard at Cal that her vision went fuzzy.

"That's not a word, and no, you're not," Merris said. "Me, I'd sit down right in front of him, snap that laptop closed, and ask about that dating site." Merris punctuated it with a sharp nod.

"Such finesse."

"It's better to get right to the point. We only have so much time. I wouldn't waste it by not getting a straight answer as soon as I figured out the question."

Merris had a point.

"Jace had to leave early. Can you go finish up the dishes, please?" She didn't want Merris whooping it up like a rodeo cowgirl when Cal spotted the heart.

But seconds later, that worry was unfounded.

Cal picked up the mug and sipped while his attention stayed glued to his laptop.

Her heart, literally and figuratively, fell apart.

28

Came in for a simple coffee, and walked out thinking that Coffee Loft is my new favorite hangout. Their merch is so cute, too. Definitely worth a trip to check out. ~ Mia

The mid-afternoon lull gave Ginger a small break. Cal was long gone. He hadn't asked to see her after all, and that weighed on her heart like an anchor was tethered to it and tossed overboard. She didn't blame him. The problem was her own doing—the storming out, the silent treatment. If she couldn't at least start a conversation, maybe she wasn't ready for a relationship with anyone.

She'd planned to give Cal the proceeds from the shelter donation box a week ago, but with his absence last week, and well... *now,* she needed to get the money off her hands *pronto.* It wasn't doing anyone any good sitting in the bank bag in her desk drawer. She'd just make a quick run over to Hearts Fur

Love. There was something else she wanted to run by Charleen anyway.

"Oh, don't trouble yourself," Charleen said on the phone when Ginger called to see if she was in. "Coming over there is the least I can do. I could use a cold brew fix anyway."

Charleen showed up half an hour later and greeted Ginger with two outstretched hands. Ginger had her drink waiting for her at an empty table, and Charleen invited Ginger to sit with her.

"Cal told me what a wonderful thing you did for us last week," Charleen said, punctuating her double handshake with a squeeze every few words. "I'm sorry I didn't get to thank you at the gala the other night. It was a whirlwind."

"I can't imagine. I'm sure you've had your mind on more important things, between that and the overall status of the shelter."

"Oh, boy. Tell me about it," she said with a shaky laugh. "Fingers crossed that something comes through. We have a couple of leads we're pursuing at the moment."

"I hope it works out." She handed Charleen the envelope of donations. "I wish it were more."

"You're a dear," she said before her eyes popped at the total written on the front of the envelope. "This was all collected at the Fall Days Festival?"

"I kept it at the counter for a few days afterward." She knew people who wanted to donate but weren't around the night of the festival.

Charleen shook her head, staring at the envelope. "Amazing."

"I doubt we would have collected so much if it wasn't for

Cal coming here every week. He's like a walking advertisement for Hearts Fur Love."

"Everyone adores him, don't they?" Charleen gushed. "And you, that was so sweet of you to take Peaches overnight. I hear she was the perfect guest."

Cal had talked about her to Charleen. Her heart flipped at the thought, wondering what else Cal shared. "I was almost tempted——"

Charleen gasped. "You were tempted to adopt her?"

"I was going to say *foster*. But no, that's probably not a good idea after all."

"Oh, but she's such a sweetheart. I can't believe she hasn't found her forever family yet." Charleen leaned forward and patted Ginger's hand. "He wrote the cutest description about her for the website. He really has a talent for that."

"He does?"

Charleen nodded. "Sometimes I read his profiles and I'm like, 'I want this dog.' As if five dogs isn't enough." She threw her head back with a hearty laugh.

"Does he write all of them?" Her pulse leapt with a little offbeat stutter.

"Most of them. I've tried, but I'm about as creative as a math book. He says that working on them is a palette cleanser for the technical writing he does all day."

"Right," she murmured as her heart sank.

He writes profiles...*for the shelter dogs*? Her mind whirled. Cal's calls had stopped today. His voicemail messages spoke of a misunderstanding. It was better to talk in person, he'd said. *To clear this up.* Now she understood what misunderstanding he referred to, and she was to blame.

But she was afraid. What if her fear of losing herself in this relationship came true? It'd happened once with Marco. She didn't want a repeat.

Cal wasn't Marco, though. She'd known that up until she read that profile, then all the doubts came rushing back, and it'd pushed her back to the starting line.

She could solve it with a simple phone call or a face-to-face conversation, yet the outcome terrified her. Still, if she let this fester any longer, Cal might truly end up writing a dating profile for himself.

He might think she wasn't worth the drama.

Too much trouble.

For a long time, she would have agreed with him. Insecurity can be exhausting, for her and for poor Cal.

It's not too late to fix things.

Oh, but maybe it was. At least until she heard his version of what she'd imagined. She prayed for a discerning heart, and that he'd be patient with her even if that was asking too much.

Like him, she took words to heart. And spoken cruelly, they could cut her to the core. It might be easy to forgive, but those words became a part of her fabric, permanently woven into her being.

And she'd hurt him. Silently accusing him of not being genuine when all he'd ever been to her was kind and generous and so delightfully charming. He made her heart sing after it had been silent for too long. She might not have accused him outright, but her indifference had wounded him.

Kind, generous, funny Cal.

But now her thoughtlessness was a part of him, too.

29

Thanks for the great coffee, delicious pastry, and the bright smiles. You're the best! ~ Fia Nicco

It'd been all he could do to not hang out on Coffee Loft's patio again today. It hadn't helped him yesterday. Ginger, if she was there at all, had stayed out of sight.

He was thankful for a full schedule today, including an initial interview with a new client. Then he'd put the finishing touches on a report to send off, and he had taken an emergency conference call to troubleshoot a network issue. He'd hung up just in time to walk the dogs, change clothes, and head to Hearts Fur Love for the monthly board meeting.

Discussing a new property acquisition for the shelter was on the agenda. Scrambling to find options, Charleen had enlisted the board members as well as volunteers to reach out to anyone with options for a new location. It was Cal's lead which looked most promising.

One of his clients was moving to a larger building across the river, and the current property included an adjacent wooded lot. He'd toured the building already with Charleen and a few of the board members, inspecting it for compatibility to retrofit their current kennels. Trouble was, buying the property would take some creative financing. The board planned another meeting within the next few days to explore loan options.

Charleen pulled out the chair next to him and sat as the meeting concluded.

"Thanks so much for everything you've done for us, Cal. I feel that I can never thank you enough. You always seem to come through for us."

"I'm happy to, you know that."

"I have a good feeling about this," she said, tapping her fist on the table. "Can you believe the gala brought in almost three times what it did last year? That's the upside of social media. And your Ginger sure is a sweetheart, collecting donations for us last week, too."

Your Ginger.

He almost corrected Charleen. *She's not my Ginger*, he wanted to say. Wishful thinking didn't make it so. But saying that sounded so final. He held out hope that Ginger just needed time, but his heart ached that he wasn't the person she sought for comfort.

"Did she bring the donations here?" With the flurry of events between the fall festival and his last-minute travels, he'd forgotten all about collecting the donations from Ginger to give to Charleen. "I'm sorry. I told her I'd get them to you."

Charleen waved away his concern. "I paid her a visit, which worked out well because it's been a minute since I've been in that cute little place. I'm still stunned she collected that much through the shop."

"Well, the word's been on the street that you need help. It's easier to fundraise when the shelter already has a strong community presence."

Charleen nudged his hand. "That's a testament to you for bringing your pups to Coffee Loft. Did I tell you that the people who adopted Rocco yesterday mentioned meeting you on the patio?"

"Rocco got adopted?" Chalk up another dog going to a forever home, thanks to Ginger's dog-friendly patio.

"He did, the lucky boy. The family has three kiddos and a big backyard, too."

Cal smiled. "All the stress and paperwork and meetings are worth it when we get news like that."

"You bet," Charleen said as she pushed up from her chair. "It's time to wrap things up here. Fingers crossed that we can make this new building ours soon."

He took out his phone on his way to the car and tapped out a message as soon as he was behind the wheel. Ginger needed to know the impact she continued to make, even by simply setting out a water dish daily and displaying the "we love dogs here" sign on the patio.

Another dog found a home because of you.

He held his breath, waiting for the dots to show that a reply was on the way.

But that was wishful thinking, too.

30

S *uper chill spot for a coffee and something sweet. Our book club has been meeting here for years, and it's always a pleasure walking into Coffee Loft where Ginger and her team greet us with smiles and the best service.* ~ The Caffeinated Bookworms

C harleen stood at the front door of Hearts Fur Love as soon as Ginger pulled into a parking space. She gave a little wave when Ginger stepped out of her car to head up the gravel walkway bordered by sedum and brown-eyed Susans in full bloom.

"Sorry to bother you two days in a row." Ginger walked inside the shelter as Charleen held the door for her. She'd meant to mention her idea to Charleen yesterday, but she'd forgotten once Charleen shared the news about Cal writing the dogs' profiles.

"Oh, it's no problem at all. You mentioned a business

proposition on the phone." Charleen said. "I hope you don't want your donation back. I've already spent it on dog food. Twenty-two fifty-pound bags, to be exact." She giggled.

Ginger paused, in part because she couldn't picture that much dog food.

Charleen's eyes popped. "Yes, you heard right."

"I'm glad it was put to good use right away." Where on earth did they keep that much food?

Charleen led her into an office. She pointed to a chair upholstered in a paisley pattern set in front of a beat-up metal desk. Glamour shots of dogs covered the wall. A wall calendar still showed the month of July. Charleen's desk was littered with paperwork, soda cans, and a half-filled mug of coffee. A peace lily with droopy leaves sat on the corner of the desk.

"I'm assuming this business proposition is related to Coffee Loft, then?" Charleen said as she pushed a bowl of peppermints toward Ginger.

Ginger took one. "Thank you. Yes, it is."

"And I'm sure you already know this, but we're a nonprofit. There's a limit on what we can do."

"I understand. That's why this might work for both of us." Ginger shifted in her seat.

"Are you and Cal in cahoots or something?"

She smiled at the word "cahoots." It'd been a minute since she was in cahoots with anyone, being one who preferred to keep to herself.

"No, this is all me. I'd like to purchase a mobile coffee truck and direct the profits solely to Hearts Fur Love for the foreseeable future."

Charleen looked at her like she waited for the punch line. Then Charleen's blank look turned to full-blown smile. "But why would you do that? Not to sound ungrateful, and I *love* that idea, but you're a businesswoman. How does this benefit you?"

"I've been lucky with my success at Coffee Loft. It's immensely satisfying to watch the joy that a simple cup of coffee brings to people." She shook her head with wonder. "But lately I've been thinking it's not enough."

Charleen nodded thoughtfully. "Tell me more."

Ginger explained how she'd long wanted to do something bigger in the way of community outreach. Getting to know Cal better and his foster work gave her direction. With her proposal, she could help the shelter *and* do what she did best: sell coffee. She'd told Charleen that the shelter wouldn't have to oversee the staff or maintain the truck; she'd take care of everything. Once expenses were covered, all income would go directly to the shelter. Having a mobile truck would also provide another training experience for her employees. She'd need to hire another crew member, but she envisioned her employees taking turns learning the mobile coffee business. This would help employees like Alice who yearned for something greater, too.

"I think this benefits my business and your shelter in equal measure. We both get more exposure."

"I've already run the idea by my attorney," Ginger explained. "Without diving in too deeply, she mentioned that's it's doable if we're careful with the language in the contract and that it syncs with your board's vision, too."

"Can you get something on paper for me to present at our next meeting?"

She nodded. "I sure will."

Charleen reached across the desk to give Ginger one of her all-encompassing handshakes. "I hope this works out. I absolutely adore this idea."

"I do, too."

Charleen's face brightened. "Are you taking ideas for names? How does *Puppa Cuppa Joe* sound?" She chortled at her own wit.

She'd been playing with names. Maybe she'd sponsor a naming contest at Coffee Loft.

When Charleen let go of her hands to jot a note, Ginger cleared her throat.

"Charleen?" She rested her elbows on the arms of the chair and leaned forward. "I could really use your help with one more thing."

31

How lucky we are to have Coffee Loft as neighbors. We love our Friday caffeine fixes. ~ Grett, Burroughs, & Petersen, LLC

Cal fastened the harness around Peaches' middle. It fit a little looser than when he'd brought her home last month. With daily walks to the park and dashing around the yard here at home, the once overweight senior dog was probably in the best shape of her life.

"Look at you, Skinny Mini. Trying to keep up with Ridley has paid off."

At the mention of his name, Ridley's ears perked up in his crate.

"Sorry, buddy. We'll do our normal walk later. Peaches has another meet-and-greet. Wish her luck."

He clipped on her leash, leading her to the door and out into the cool, blue-sky November day.

Charleen had called the night before to report that someone else was interested in Peaches and asked if he could meet in Fox Ridge Park at ten this morning.

As he walked Peaches underneath the stone arch leading into the small, tree-shaded park four blocks away, his thoughts turned to Ginger again. Three days after the gala, and he still hadn't heard from her. He'd stopped leaving messages. If she wanted anything to do with him, she knew how to get a hold of him. Whatever she thought he did was unfounded. The pain of being misunderstood wasn't near as great as what she probably felt reading that profile on his laptop. Not after what her ex put her through. He held onto the hope that she'd reach out to him when she felt ready.

He parked himself on a bench near the little stream that ran through this corner of the park. While Peaches explored a bed of decaying asters behind him, he checked his emails. It wasn't very long before he heard footsteps crunching the fallen leaves at the same time that Peaches tugged on her leash.

Before he could turn around, the scent of vanilla and coffee beans almost made his heart stop. He jumped to his feet just as she walked around the front of the bench, and they collided.

"Ginger." He steadied her by grabbing her arms.

"Hi there."

The shock of seeing her set his pulsing drumming a whole new rhythm, but she didn't seem as surprised to see him.

"What are you doing here?"

She looked down at Peaches, who'd done an admirable

job of tying them both up in her leash. A step in any direction would send one or both of them crashing to the pavement.

"I've come for a meet-and-greet." She scratched Peaches underneath her chin with one hand as she unwound the nylon web around their legs. "Can we sit?"

He was so confused by her sudden appearance and by the knowledge that she'd arranged this meeting through Charleen that words failed him. What was happening? He backed up to the bench again and sat.

"I'm so sorry it's taken me so long to...get back to you." Her brows knitted together in apology when she looked at him. "I've had a lot to sort through the last few days."

He nodded, hoping that that time had worked in his favor.

"And you're okay?" he asked, even though what he really wanted to know is if they'd survived.

Ginger's uneven breath punctuated the silence for a few moments.

"I am," she said finally.

"What happened, Ginger?"

Her eyes dipped to her lap and she swallowed.

"I saw the profile on your laptop that night. It was totally by accident." She explained about spilling her drink and moving the laptop to clean up the mess. "My mind immediately flew to the worst possible scenario, and I couldn't think straight."

"You know differently now, right?"

Ginger clamped down on her lips, nodding. Her eyes glistened as she let her gaze sweep over his face.

"I'm so sorry, Cal. For how I just disappeared. For not

sorting it out sooner. For thinking of myself and not what you were going through."

"*Whoa, whoa.* Don't apologize for that. I get it, Ginger. You're not selfish. Considering what this Marco guy put you through, it's called self-preservation."

She let out a little sob before clamping a hand over her mouth. But her shoulders still shook, so he gathered her in his arms and rubbed her back while she cried into the folds of his coat. Peaches, not to be forgotten, hopped onto the bench and curled up next to Ginger.

They stayed like that for a while until the only sounds he heard were sniffles and sighs. She rummaged in her coat pockets for a tissue, but he produced one from his own first and handed it over. She smiled up at him through teary green eyes, and the crack in his heart healed in an instant.

"It's such a relief," she said as they faced each other again. She dabbed the tissue underneath each eye, trying to catch any wayward tears.

"What is?"

"To know why I wasn't ready for a relationship after Marco."

He waited.

"I'd been too busy hiding to confront the pain. I figured I could ignore it and it'd magically disappear. For a long time, I thought it did. Until you came along."

He lifted her hand to kiss the palm. "It doesn't work like that. Connecting the dots from your past to your future is the only way to heal."

She stared at him. "That's perfect. I never thought of it that way."

He shrugged with a smile. "My mom is a wise woman."

"I'd like to meet her someday."

"That can be arranged." He laid his arm across the back of the bench and drew her closer.

Ginger cupped his face in her hands and gazed at him with so much emotion that he nearly stopped breathing.

"Thank you for being patient with me," she said.

"I didn't have a choice," he breathed. "You've completely and profoundly captured my heart. I'm kind of broken without you."

"I love the sound of that," she murmured as she closed the space between their lips.

The nibble on his bottom lip was barely discernible, but it sent a river of delight rushing up his spine. The ache of their separation made this reunion that much sweeter. He pulled Ginger closer, tucking her under his arm where she fit like she'd been made especially for the spot. Her hands cupped either side of his face, claiming him, and he was powerless under her spell. As they kissed, his head swam as she overwhelmed his senses. The sight of her, the scent of her perfume, the soft warmth of her skin. It was all too much.

Reluctantly, he pulled away a moment later to ask what had just popped into his head.

"Now what are you going to tell poor Peaches about using her to get to me today?"

She smiled down at Peaches who still rested on the bench next to her, curled into a tight ball in peaceful doggie repose.

"I came to *ask* her if she'd like to come live with Daisy and me."

He waited for her to laugh and tell him she was just kidding, but Ginger was serious.

"Daisy called a meeting yesterday." She tried to hide a smirk, but failed.

"A meeting for two?"

"Yep. Basically, the only item on the agenda was 'Adopt Peaches.' I didn't have a say in the matter."

"Tyrannical bosses are awful to work for."

"The worst," she whispered.

"I bet you're not one, are you?" He wrapped his arms around her shoulders again, as she looked up at him, smiling.

She shrugged. "You'll have to ask the crew at Coffee Loft," she purred, studying his lips.

"I'd rather just take my chances here," he said as he luxuriated in the feeling of her lips' velvety softness on his chin.

"That can be arranged."

32

've visited Coffee Loft more times than I can remember, but I'm finally taking the time to write a review. I wish I could give it more than five stars. Yes, it's that phenomenal. This place consistently delivers the best coffee and pastries. I'm so lucky to have them right down the block. ~ A Forever Fan

A week after Ginger brought Peaches back into her home, this time for good, she, Cal, and the three animals got together for a movie night at her place.

Ginger kicked up her legs to rest her crossed ankles on the coffee table. Her laptop sat on her thighs. She needed to place an order for syrups—like, *yesterday*—but first she needed a dose of positive affirmation.

In the kitchen, Cal fetched the bag of popcorn from the microwave. The buttery aroma filled Ginger's apartment, competing with the hot chocolate he'd already whipped up for both of them.

While he emptied the popcorn into a bowl, his audience waited patiently.

"The three of you are pathetic," he said, looking down at the floor.

Though the kitchen counter limited the view at Cal's feet, it wasn't hard to imagine the three sets of eyes studying his every move. Ridley, Peaches, and Daisy—the latter of whom had been adopting the habits of begging and shaking paws from her canine friends—waited for kernels to drop. Sidestepping his rapt audience, Cal brought her a mug of hot chocolate, his own special concoction of chili powder, cayenne, and orange zest added to the mix. She'd raved about it the first time he made it for her. It was a small consolation for not being chosen for the Forty Under Forty's top spot. She'd learned the results earlier that day.

"You sure know how to make a girl feel better."

"I take my job very seriously," Cal said as he sank into the couch beside her. She met his lips as he leaned in, and a tingle of delight coursed through her when he kissed her.

"I'm going to recommend you for a promotion," she said, breathing in the scent of his sandalwood cologne, the chocolate on his breath.

"Are you sure you can handle that?"

His kisses traveled across her cheek to her neck as she turned back to her laptop. But she closed her eyes, finding it hard to focus.

"What are you looking at?" he asked, his words a soft hum against her skin.

"Reading a few reviews always makes me feel better."

"I'm glad it's that simple," he purred.

"And this, of course." She leaned her head against his forehead. The soft texture of his lips made her head spin.

Cal sat up. "Okay, I'll stop," he teased, slipping his arm behind her.

"Don't stop on my account." She gave him a sidelong glance, caressing his cheek, then held up her mug. "We need to celebrate your success, though. To Hearts Fur Love's new digs."

He clinked his mug against hers. "Thank you. What a relief it is that the site worked out. Now to move thirty kennels and just as many dogs by the end of the month."

She sipped the drink, then set it on the side table. "Will you have enough hands?"

He nodded. "I think we'll have more than enough. People are stepping up like crazy."

Ginger looked back at her laptop. Her habit of reading positive reviews to lift her spirits was good medicine. She'd discovered this years ago when she first opened Coffee Loft, needing quick pick-me-ups amid the uncertainty and chaos of being a brand-new business owner. It was cheap therapy.

"Listen to this new one: 'Coffee Lovers, listen up. If you're looking for your new favorite coffeehouse, look no further than Coffee Loft in Greenhaven. Whether you're a one-drink kind of person—' Hey, that sounds like you."

"I do like my café au laits," he said.

"'—or like to sample everything on the menu, you won't be disappointed with what this gem has to offer. And what's not to love about a place who celebrates local artists? Seriously, check out the rotating gallery of works on the walls which change monthly. My most favorite spot in the Quad City area."

"Have you ever received a *bad* review?" he asked while his attention was still on her screen.

"Sure. Plenty."

"Those people seriously aren't right."

She shrugged. "We're not perfect. I use those reviews to improve if they're constructive. If they're mean, I ignore."

"That's a good policy." He rubbed her shoulder.

"Oh, I forgot to tell you. I think I found a trailer."

"Does it need work, or will it be coffee-ready?"

The little Mini Winnie had been slightly damaged in a fender bender, she'd been told at the dealership where she'd seen it listed. After having it inspected by an independent body shop, they'd given her the thumbs up to purchase. Only cosmetic damage—and minor at that—nothing structural. They'd begin work on it as soon as she hired someone with a hitch to haul it into town.

"It needs a little sprucing up. Some of the siding needs replacing, then after the paint job, it'll be ready for business. Brad at City Collision gave me a great quote."

"He's a gem. The best. Hands down the top mechanic in the Quad Cities."

She stared at him, suppressing a smile.

"What?" he asked.

"What you just said."

Cal looked perplexed. "That he's the top mechanic?"

"No, before that. Is it you?" It couldn't be.

"What are you talking about?"

His praise sounded so similar to—

She scrolled through the review section on Coffee Loft's page, stopping on one as laughter tickled her throat. There. "'A Quad City gem,'" she read aloud.

Cal's brows ticked up. "What about it?"

She searched some more. "How about this one: 'I love this gem of a place.'"

There were so many. She could almost hear Cal's voice replacing her own as she read them.

"'There are gems and then there is Coffee Loft.'" She snapped her laptop closed and looked at him. He still wore that innocent look. "You use that word a lot. You wrote a lot of these reviews, didn't you?"

He pointed at himself and mouthed "me?"

"Yes, you. Don't tell me it's not you." She couldn't love him any more than she did at that moment. She set her laptop on the coffee table.

"If I admit it, will you still love me?" he asked, hooking his hands behind his head, puffing his chest out, and wearing one of his irresistible side smirks. If Cal truly doubted her love for him, his confidence didn't get the memo.

She looped her arms around his neck, and he took that as a cue to hug her close. Their noses touched as she looked him in the eye.

"Even more than I do now."

"You got me, then. Guilty," he murmured as he raised his hand.

"How can I help but love you, Cal Donner?"

He chuckled. "Believe me, I asked myself that same question for a very long time."

"Thank goodness I finally came around, huh?"

He answered her with a kiss that left no doubt about how grateful he was that she did.

Epilogue - Thirteen Months Later

ny visit to Coffee Loft is a treat, whether it happens at the beginning of your day, or at the end. ~ Merry Hill

A freshly cut Douglas fir towering above them in Cal's living room stood as a noble audience to the chaos playing out around it. She and Cal sat cross-legged on the floor in front of it on Christmas Eve amidst a flurry of animals and torn wrapping paper.

Ridley, giddy with a new beef bone, dashed around the room with Peaches in hot pursuit. Ornaments swung on the tree branches each time they completed a lap around the room's perimeter. Daisy, who'd pawed at Peaches' bag of doggie dental sticks earlier, had secretly carried the package onto the highest shelf flanking the fireplace. The cat looked down at the mayhem in willful disdain while tearing into the bag. Bits of packaging floated to the floor like metallic blue snowflakes.

Ginger pulled back the tissue paper of Cal's gifts for Daisy and Peaches, smiling at the matching turquoise dog and cat collars studded with rhinestones nestled in the bottom of the box. She held them up, barely able to contain a laugh.

"Daisy and Peaches will love these, I'm sure." She nodded to the gift next to Cal. "Now open Ridley's."

Cal let out a whoop when he unwrapped Ridley's gift. A much larger dog collar, purple with a dangling silver paw charm, was inscribed with "Coffee and Canines—the Pawfect Blend."

"Great minds think alike," he said, turning it over in his hands. Cal called over Ridley and switched out his collar. Once Cal snapped it in place, the dog seemed to know he wore a slicker version of the old one, judging by the jaunty steps he took between Cal and his dog bed to get back to his new bone.

"Now I feel bad. Maybe I should have their collars inscribed, too," he said. "How about 'Coffee and Cats—the Purrfect Blend' for Daisy?"

She chuckled. "Daisy would be offended. She doesn't want to be paired with anything. She's an independent woman."

"Of course, she is." He rolled his eyes before his gaze settled on her again. He took her hand, grinning as he looked down and clasped his fingers between hers. "Speaking of independent women, I was at a loss when it came time to shop for you."

A pang of disappointment pinched her insides. She'd had trouble shopping for him, too, but she finally settled on a smart mug so his coffee at home never went cold. She'd had it personalized, too. It wasn't anything elegant; he was admittedly a practical guy.

"That's okay. I didn't really expect—"

He brought his hand out from around his back. "So I bought the one I liked best and told the jeweler I might be exchanging it...er, *we* might be exchanging it for something you'll love more."

The little black box with a silver crown etched into the lid wasn't even opened yet and she was already nodding her head yes. Happy tears blurred her vision so much that when she looked up at Cal, he was all wavy, as if a vintage pane of glass stood between them.

"I looked at three different stores, and this is the closest I could find to something as beautiful as you." He got off the floor and reached for her to pull her up, too. When she was on her feet, he chuckled as he plucked the ring from its velvet-lined resting place.

"Will you marry me, Ginger?"

A teardrop diamond ring surrounded by a halo of smaller diamonds winked at her. She swallowed the lump that had risen in her throat as she looked up at him, and found him struggling to keep the smile contained to his face. He looked near to bursting, his cheeks plumped with the widest grin, as he slipped it onto her finger.

Ginger threw her arms around his neck, burying her face into his collar.

"Yes," she breathed. It was the only word she could

manage at the moment. Her throat constricted, and a little happy sob escaped.

"Is it too big? I'll take it back. I had no idea what I was doing, and the guy kept bringing out more and more until I was totally flustered, but then I felt a little pressured because the place got busy while I was in there, and...this was the one I picked." He said all of this into her hair, and she couldn't keep from laughing at his excited babbling.

"It's what I would've picked, too," she finally said in a throaty whisper, pulling away so she could see how perfect it looked on her hand.

His brows knitted together. "Really?"

She nodded and dabbed at the tears pricking the corners of her eyes. "Really."

Cal cupped her face between his hands and brushed her lips with a kiss.

"You have no idea how much I love you," he whispered as he rested his forehead against hers. "If you knew even a fraction of the amount, it might scare you."

"Never. It would just make me want more." She pulled him into a hug again and splayed her fingers over his shoulder to marvel at the ring, at what it symbolized.

Together. For a lifetime.

"I wouldn't complain," he said.

They walked over to the front window. Cal shut off the lamp, and they stared at the wintry scene outside. Freshly fallen snow and a full moon lit the lawn with a dazzling luminescence. Daisy must have sensed the momentous occasion because she leapt down from the shelf, landing on the armchair behind Cal. She placed her two paws on his hip, as if bestowing her blessing on the happy arrangement.

Cal shifted to scratch Daisy's head.

She suppressed a laugh. "I think she's asking about her role in the wedding already."

"She'll insist on being in charge of something, I'm sure," he said.

"How about keeping you as close to me as possible?"

Cal looped an arm around her waist, drawing her closer, and kissed her again. It fired every nerve ending in her body. She couldn't imagine a time in the future when it wouldn't.

Future.

That seemed so surreal, so perfect.

His eyes burned into her when he drew back.

"That, Future-Mrs.-Donner, should never be a problem."

Cal's Spicy Hot Chocolate

6 cups skim milk
3 tablespoons unsweetened cocoa powder
3 tablespoons white sugar
1 teaspoon vanilla extract
1 teaspoon cinnamon
1/2 teaspoon chili powder
1/2 teaspoon ground nutmeg
1/4 teaspoon ground cloves
Cinnamon sticks (optional)

In a saucepan, heat milk on low until lukewarm. Mix cocoa powder and sugar into milk until dissolved. Add vanilla, cinnamon, chili powder, nutmeg, and cloves. Stir occasionally for a few more minutes until well combined. Serve with a cinnamon stick.

Enjoy!

Welcome Back to Coffee Loft

Welcome back to The Coffee Loft, where a new round of stories has been brewed especially for you.

Those of you stopping by to visit again, we've missed you. The feeling of home is the same that you loved before. If it's your first time, prepare to be swept off your feet. While our menu hasn't changed, we think you'll be pleased with the fall favorites we've added. Fans of pumpkin spiced lattes, peppermint mochas, and rich, chocolaty cocoas will not be disappointed. This multi-author collection of stand-alone sweet romcoms is filled to the brim with the swoons you love and adore. From sweet kisses to grand gestures and matchmaking surprises, each mug and story will be filled with everything you crave.

So come on in and let us serve you with that happy ever after you've come to expect.

Find the entire collection here: Coffee Loft Fall Collection

While you are at it, visit the first collection here.

A Special Note to Readers

Thank you for reading *A Cafe Au Lait Kind of Love*. I hope you enjoyed Ginger's and Cal's story as much as I loved writing it. If you'd like up-to-date news about other books I'm writing, join my newsletter Welcome to the Sweet Life. You'll also get access to free content as well as subscriber-only giveaways, sneak peeks at new stories, and exclusive contests.

And, of course, if you enjoyed the book, I would love for you to leave a review on Amazon and/or Goodreads!

Happy Reading!

Dawn

Also by D.E. Malone

Hearts in Hendricks series

Love Like Water

Love Like Fire

Love Like Air

Love Like Forever

Blueberry Point Romance series

Love, Lies and Lavender

Love, Lies and Mistletoe

Love, Lies and Lullabies

Love, Lies and Lemon Pie

Love, Lies and Sleigh Rides

Love, Lies and Valentines

Love, Lies and Literature

Blueberry Point Romance Collection (four novellas)

Port Chance series

That Woman on Thistledown Lane

Apple Blossom Dreams

A Forever Kiss in Silver Leaf Falls

Acknowledgments

To my fellow Coffee Loft Authors J.P., Amy, Ellie, Kerry, Susanne, Tia, TJ, Mel, Tracy, Meg, Kimberley, H.M., and Bella - I'm ecstatic to be a part of this Fall Collection with you people. Your talent, enthusiasm, and generosity are infectious. A special shout-out to J.P. and Amy for dreaming up this adorable series and for the months of organizing it took to get this series off the ground (pun intended).

Rachael Bloome - Thank you so much for reading what I sent your way, even when our schedules didn't quite mesh. Your insight and gracious comments truly made this a much better story.

Marisa Figueiredo - I'm so thrilled that we continue to work together. I'm amazed at what you can see when I hand over a manuscript. Here's to many more of my books that will land in your inbox.

Sarah West - Thank you for your patience while my comma handicap continues to confound me. Seriously, I appreciate all that you see and question and correct in my stories. It's such a relief to send off a manuscript to you and have it come back so tidy.

Renee Dennis Simmons - Thank you for coming up with the name for Hearts Fur Love Dog Rescue. I knew it was the perfect name the second I saw your suggestion.

For the ARC readers who read the early version before it went public, for pointing out the little things that go unnoticed, for taking time to leave reviews, and offering support in general. A special thanks to MaryEllen who's my final last-pass person and also the fastest reader I know!

For Dave, Hayley, Jack, Josh, Brandon, and the Three Ees for your continued love and support of my writing life.

Finally, to the animal rescue organizations who offer their tireless dedication in finding forever homes for the animals that come under their care. The work you do is inspiring, through the joy and heartbreak, and is so very much appreciated. I'd also like to acknowledge Wishbone Canine Rescue, Humane Society of Central Illinois, and Best Friends Animal Society, all of whom my family and I have personally worked with and volunteered for, and from which we've adopted the very best doggos.

About the Author

D.E. Malone writes sweet contemporary small-town romance and is the author of the Hearts in Hendricks, Blueberry Point Romance, and Port Chance series. Her work has appeared in the Chicken Soup for the Soul series, *Highlights for Children*, and other publications. When not writing, she loves the outdoors—gardening, hiking, and exploring places off-the-beaten path. She lives in central Illinois with her husband.